FROM THE
DESK OF THE EDITOR

Dear Reader,

There are some books that you never want to end—that you remember long after the last page is turned. For me, *An Accidental Woman* is that kind of book. It's not a typical romance, but rather a poignant and affecting story about love as experienced by two couples who live in a picturesque New England town. One couple savors the incredible magic of falling in love, while another couple reaches a crossroads when their long-standing love is put to the test. The powerful ending brought tears to my eyes—and what could be a higher recommendation than that?

Happy reading,

Paula Marchese

Paula Marchese
Editor

An Accidental Woman

Barbara Delinsky

SELECTED AND EDITED BY READER'S DIGEST

THE WEEKEND READER

GREAT ESCAPES
Mysteries, romances, thrillers, and family dramas

ACTION-PACKED
Thrillers, adventures, and mysteries

MUST READS
Bestsellers, reviewers' choices,
exciting debuts, and word-of-mouth favorites

THOUGHT-PROVOKING
Critically acclaimed popular fiction and
nonfiction, current affairs, and biographies

To change your choice of categories or number of books,
call us at 1-800-316-9838.

This condensation has been created by The Reader's Digest Association, Inc., by special arrangement with Simon & Schuster, Inc.

The original edition of *An Accidental Woman* was published at $25.00 by Simon & Schuster, Inc.

Printed in the United States of America

An Accidental Woman

Chapter One

Within seconds of coming awake, Micah Smith felt a chill at the back of his neck that had nothing to do with the cold air seeping in through the window cracked open by his side of the bed. It was barely dawn. He didn't have to glance past Heather's body toward the nightstand clock to know that, but could see it in the purpling that preceded daylight when February snows covered the forest floor.

The purpling seemed deeper this morning, but that wasn't what caused his alarm. Nor was it any sound from the girls' room.

No. What held him totally still, eyes on that inch of open window, was the sound that came from beyond. Even in winter the woods were filled with live things, but what he heard now was neither deer nor owl. It was a car, moving slowly down the snow-crusted drive toward the house that Micah had built for his family.

Get out of bed, cried a silent voice, but he remained inert. Barely breathing, he listened. Not one car. Two. They inched their way closer, then stopped. Their engines went still.

Do something, cried that silent voice, more urgent now. But he couldn't move, other than to turn his head toward Heather. She continued to sleep, oblivious to what he heard.

As he watched the swirl of her long dark hair, touched by a generous dusting of silver, he heard the stealthy click of car doors. A patch of Heather's pale shoulder showed through the tangle of her hair. He would have touched it if he hadn't feared waking her, but he didn't want that. Once she was awake, once she heard what he heard, once this moment ended, their lives would be changed. He didn't know how he knew that, but he did.

The footsteps coming toward the house were careful, making only the occasional crunch on the snow, but a lifetime of living in the New Hampshire woods had trained Micah's ear well. A soft knock came at the front door. Micah quickly slipped from under the thick down comforter. Silently he pulled on jeans and left the bedroom. In seconds he was down the hall and through the living room. He pulled the door open before another knock came, though Pete Duffy's hand was already raised.

Pete was second-in-command to Lake Henry's police chief, William Jacobs, and he was a friend of Micah's, which was certainly why he'd been chosen to come. The authorities would want things kept calm. A second man stood just behind Pete on the front porch. Micah didn't know this man or the two women who were with him. All three wore jeans and identical blue jackets that Micah knew must have law-enforcement initials on the back.

"We need Heather," Pete said in an apologetic whisper, jutting his chin toward the threesome with him. "They have a warrant."

Micah swallowed. A warrant was serious. "For what?"

The man with Pete extended both hands. One held paperwork, the other his ID. "Jim Mooney. FBI. I have a warrant for the arrest of Heather Malone on charges of flight to avoid prosecution."

Micah considered the man's words. He had always known that Heather hid her past. During those times when he had wondered what might have caused her secretiveness, involvement with the law had been a worst-case scenario. Now he could only pray that the charges against her were of the not-so-serious kind, though he feared those wouldn't have brought the FBI to his doorstep at dawn.

"Prosecution for what?" he asked the agent.

"Murder."

A sharp breath escaped Micah—oddly, he felt relief. If murder was the charge, then there surely was a mistake. "That's impossible. Heather's incapable of murder."

"Maybe as Heather Malone. But we have evidence that her real name is Lisa Matlock and that fifteen years ago she killed a man in California."

"Heather's never been in California."

"Lisa has," the agent informed him. "She grew up there. She was there until fifteen years ago, when she deliberately ran a man down with her car. She disappeared afterward. Your Heather arrived in Lake Henry fourteen years ago and worked as a short-order cook, just like Lisa did in California. Heather's face is identical to Lisa's, down to the gray eyes and the scar at the corner of the mouth."

"There are millions of women with gray eyes," Micah said, "and that scar came from a car accident." The words were barely out when he realized what he'd said. But the agent absolved him.

"Not this one. She escaped this accident unscathed, but

the man she ran down died—a man she tried to extort minutes before she ran him down."

Micah snorted. "Not Heather. I don't care what name she uses. She's gentle and kind. She'd die herself before she'd kill someone."

"If that's true, it'll come out in a trial. For now, I need her to come out here. Either you bring her to us, or we go in."

"You can't do that," Micah said, straightening his six-foot-four frame. "This is my house."

Pete stepped between the two men and told Micah, "They have a warrant. That gives them the right to take her. Don't rile them."

A low light suddenly came on behind him, a lamp near the spot where the living room met the hall. Heather stood there. She had slipped on a robe. As she looked at the people beyond the door, her eyes grew wider. Micah turned to look at her. Those eyes weren't just gray; they were iridescent. They held his in a silent plea.

Micah went to Heather and searched her eyes for a sign of knowledge or guilt. "They say you're someone else," he whispered. "They must be wrong, but they need you to go with them."

"Where?" she asked with barely a sound.

"I don't know," he murmured. "Maybe to Willie Jake's office."

The two female agents approached. "We need to book her," one told him before turning to Heather. "We'll go with you to dress."

Heather's eyes flew from one woman's face to the other, then to Micah's. She put a hand on his chest, anchoring her now against the terror that had seized her.

"*I'll* take her to dress," he said, but one of the agents was already grasping her arm and reciting her Miranda rights.

Frantic to help her but knowing he was hamstrung, Micah glanced at Pete. "Someone's gonna answer for this. It's wrong."

Pete came forward as the two female agents ushered Heather down the hall. "I told them that. So'd Willie Jake. He spent most of last night trying to talk some sense into them, but they have the warrant, Micah. It's legal. There's nothing we can do."

Micah turned back to Heather, but she had disappeared into the bedroom.

"Daddy?" came a soft voice from even farther down the hall.

Micah turned in alarm. It was Melissa, his seven-year-old daughter. In a voice that was as normal as he could make it, he said, "Go back to bed, Missy. Too early to get up."

But Missy, by far the more curious and bold of his two girls, padded toward him in her long pink nightgown. Her hair was as dark as his—and as thick and long as Heather's—but wildly curly. "Why's Pete here?" she asked.

"Uh, he has to ask Heather some questions. Now, I want you to go back to bed. Make sure your sister sleeps a little longer."

"She's awake. She's just scared to come out."

Micah knew it wasn't as simple as Star being scared. He had long since accepted that the five-year-old possessed an odd adult insight. Star would know something was wrong. Her fear would be real.

"Then go back in and play with her. That'll make her feel better."

Missy flattened herself against the wall, her expression defiant, as Heather emerged from the bedroom with the two female agents. She was dressed in jeans and a heavy sweater. When she caught sight of Missy, her eyes met Micah's for a single, alarmed second.

Micah said, "Go on back in with Star, Missy. I need you to help."

Missy stayed pressed against the wall.

Heather knelt by her side. "Daddy's right, sweetie," she said in a gentle voice. "Go in with Star. She needs you."

Defiance gone, replaced by worry, Missy slipped an arm around Heather's shoulder. "Where are you going?"

"Into town."

"When'll you be back?"

"A little later."

"Do you promise?"

Waiting for the answer himself—hanging his future on it much as the child was—Micah saw Heather swallow. "Yes. I'll do my best to be here when you get home from school," she whispered. She closed her eyes, and a look of anguish crossed her face. As she came toward him, her eyes filled with tears. When she was as close as she could be, she whispered, "Call Cassie."

Cassie Byrnes, a lawyer, was one of Heather's closest friends.

When the two female agents ushered Heather toward the door, Micah kept pace behind them. "Where are you taking her?"

Mooney stepped in his path as the agents whisked Heather outside. "Concord. She'll go before a magistrate there this morning."

"Is she being charged with murder?"

"No. They'll ask for extradition. Heather can waive an extradition hearing and go back with them, or she can fight it. They can't take her back—can't charge her with murder or anything else—until they make a solid enough case that the charges are legit."

Micah trotted barefoot down the steps, oblivious to the

crusted ice on the wood planks. He watched Heather vanish into the back of a dark van, and then he began to run. "I want to go with her."

Pete ran alongside him. "Not wise to do that right now. They won't let you. You'd be better going down later with Cassie."

But when Pete pulled at Micah's arm and tried to steer him back to the house, Micah tugged free and ran on. He stopped at the closed door of the van, bent down, and flattened a hand on the window. His eyes met Heather's just as the engine started, and short of running alongside until the van gained enough speed to leave him behind, he had no choice but to stay. Straightening, he stared at the head looking back at him. He held that gaze until the van rounded a bend and disappeared down the forest drive. She was gone.

Suddenly he felt cold inside and out. He started back toward the house. Only Pete's Lake Henry cruiser was left. "Some friend you are," he muttered as he stormed past the deputy.

"Micah, what could we do?" Pete cried, following him. "They had the warrant."

"You could have called us. Warned us."

"How would that've helped? Would you have run off, like you were guilty of something? This was the only way, Micah."

Micah took the front steps in twos, energized by anger.

"Look at it this way," Pete said. "They have to *prove* she is who they say. You think anyone here's going to say she's someone else? No way. So they're going to have to dig up other people. That'll take some time, don't you think?"

What Micah thought was that *any* amount of time he was separated from Heather was bad. He wanted her with him, and not just for the girls' sake. He had come to depend on her gentleness, her sureness. He was a nuts-and-bolts guy who sometimes was so focused on the small details that he didn't see the larger picture. Heather did. She was his helpmate when it came to being human. She was also his partner when it came to maple sugaring, and the season was about to start.

Striding into the house, he shut the door before Pete could follow. Missy stood in the middle of the living room looking crushed. There was no sign of Star. Micah looked behind and under the sofa, the chairs, the coffee table, but it wasn't until he looked behind him at the bookshelves flanking the front door that he spotted her. She was on the bottom shelf, tucked in beside a stack of *National Geographic* magazines that were a stark yellow against the pale green of her nightie. Her knees were drawn up and held close by her small arms. Her eyes were woefully sad and knowing.

His heart lurched. It wasn't that he had stronger feelings for Star, just that he worried more about her. She was more serious than Melissa. Whereas Missy said what she thought, Star was quieter. She'd been an infant when her mother had left—"left" being the word he used in place of "skidded off the road, went down a ravine, and burned up in the cab of her truck." He knew Star couldn't. Hunkering down, he caught up the child and said, "Everything's okay," as he carried her down the hall to the room the girls shared. He set her on her bed, a mess of gingham sheets, pillow, and down. "But you can help me out now. I need you and your sister to get dressed while I make some calls. Then we'll have breakfast."

"We won't wait for Momma," the child said in a sure little voice.

"No. She'll have breakfast in town."

"What'll she eat?"

He thought for a minute. "Eggs? Waffles? If we eat the same thing, it'll be like she's with us. What do you think?"

"Maybe."

"Oatmeal's her favorite," Missy announced from close by. "She'd be having that. But I'll only eat it if it has lots of maple sugar on it."

"Well, we have lots of maple sugar, so we're golden. Help your sister dress," Micah said, and with a return of the urgency he felt when the FBI van disappeared with Heather inside, he headed for the room opposite the girls'. He had added this room soon after Heather moved in, hoping it would be for a child they would have together, but they'd been too busy, it seemed, growing the girls, growing the business. To reach the closet, he had to step over the dollhouse village he'd made for the girls.

The knapsack was on a shelf out of reach of the girls and far to the right, well hidden by clothes and boxes. A drab, brown thing, the knapsack was small and worn. To Micah's knowledge it was the only relic Heather had of her pre–Lake Henry days.

Tucking the sack under his arm—and refusing to consider what was inside—Micah went through the kitchen to the back hall. Stepping into his boots, he pulled on a jacket and stuffed the knapsack inside. He went out, down the back steps, and over the well-packed snow on an oft-trodden path. The sugarhouse stood several hundred feet up the hill. It was a long stone building with a large cupola on top. Micah slipped inside and shut the door behind him. He went through the main room, past yards of stainless steel equipment to the far end, where wood was stacked high and deep. The wood here was only a fraction of what he would use when the season began. The rest lay outside, beyond the large double doors. At the rear end of the inside stack, he pulled off three logs, tucked the bag into the pile, put the logs back. Then he left the shed.

Back in the kitchen, he called Cassie Byrnes.

• • •

Cassie rarely slept late. Five hours a night was all she needed. Since her husband, Mark, and their three children were all excellent sleepers, she regularly used the early morning hours for work.

This morning she was doing town business. In the annual election, she had been renamed chairman of the Lake Henry Committee—for the fifth year in a row—which should have been shocking, since she was a woman and barely thirty-six, distinctly different from the older men who had traditionally run the town. But times had begun to change. A lifelong resident who was articulate and effective, Cassie was also on the correct side of the environmental issues that were the committee's major concern. Most often these had to do with the loons that arrived each April, nested, and raised their young well into November. They were gone for the winter now, flown east to fish blissfully in unfrozen seacoast waters. There were many in town who, fearing for the integrity of the lake, wanted to add security in the form of three police officers, one cruiser, and the appropriate testing equipment to steadily monitor the condition of the lake. Unfortunately, these additions cost money. Cassie was currently trying to determine exactly how much.

The telephone rang. Eyes flying to the clock, she caught up the receiver. It was six thirty in the morning. This was no pleasure call.

"This is Cassie," she said quietly.

The voice on the other end was low and tight. "It's Micah. They arrested Heather. We need your help."

"What are you talking about? Who arrested her?"

"The FBI. They say she has a whole other identity and that she killed someone before she moved here. Flight to avoid prosecution—that's what they're charging her with. Then there's murder. And extortion. Pete was here, saying the whole thing was legal."

Cassie remained numb for a minute. Heather was her friend. She was the last person in town whom Cassie would have thought to be in trouble with the law. "Where have they taken her?"

"Concord, I think. They said there'd be a hearing this morning."

"Not until I'm there to represent her," Cassie declared with a certain indignation. "Let me find out for sure where she is; then you and I will take a ride. Pick me up in fifteen minutes?"

"Yup."

Chapter Two

Poppy Blake was awake, lying on her side, facing the windows. Anyone looking in would have thought she was watching dawn creep over the lake, because it was a breathtaking sight. Snow lay pristine over ice eighteen inches thick. Tall hemlocks and pines formed a shadowed skyscape on the islands that dotted the lake. As day arrived, a swath of brightening light climbed behind their limbs.

Poppy saw none of it. Her mind was miles away, in a dream place where one could erase mistakes of the past and start fresh. In that place, she wasn't lying in bed alone. Nor, in her dream place, was there a wheelchair by the bed.

Poppy's legs didn't work. They hadn't since a snowmobile accident twelve years before. In those twelve years she had learned everything there was to know about life as a paraplegic—the most important lesson being that she couldn't turn back the clock.

Still, there were times when she dreamed. This morning's fantasy involved a man she'd seen only a handful of times. He was five ten, had red hair, blue eyes, and a sexy baritone. He called her regularly—or used to, until she put him off one time too many. What choice did she have? She couldn't keep up with him from a wheelchair. Apparently, he'd come to agree. He hadn't called in a month.

The phone on her bedstand rang now—a single line, far removed from the complex system in the other room that Poppy used for business. She ran a telephone answering service for Lake Henry and the neighboring towns and sat for much of the day before a large bank of buttons, directing calls from one place to the next, taking messages for the townsfolk, passing on information. While family and friends used the personal line, they never called this early.

In the seconds that it took to reach the receiver, she had horrid visions of her mother being ill. But the number that was illuminated on the handset wasn't from Florida, where Maida was spending January, February, and March. It was a local number. Heather's.

"Hey?" she said, half greeting, half asking, wondering why her friend would be calling so early when they'd been together the night before. But Heather wasn't on the other end.

"It's Micah. There's trouble." His next words blurred—made no sense to her at all—until he said, "I need someone to get the girls to school. Can you do it? I'm worried about Star."

Poppy pictured the little girl with long hair framing pale skin and deep-set dark eyes. "Of course I can do it," she told him, confused. "But Heather isn't someone else. What are you talking about?"

"I'm not talking about anything. It's the FBI that's saying it."

"*Killed* someone? I don't think so. We've been friends since she first came to town. She went through my accident with me, and she couldn't have been more giving or understanding. Heather couldn't kill anyone if she tried."

"That's what I said, but I don't count. I'll be there in five minutes, okay?"

"I'll be at the door."

And she was. Poppy was a minimalist. She didn't bother with fancy clothes or makeup, rarely had, even before the accident. A quick trip to the bathroom, where everything was perfectly situated for wheelchair access, was all she allowed herself this morning.

On the porch, draped in a parka, she combed her pixie-short hair with her fingers as she watched the headlights of Micah's truck approach. The road was narrow but paved, the latter being one of the concessions that Poppy had made when, soon after the accident, her parents had carved off a wedge of their own land to build her a house. The ramp from the porch had heat coils underneath that enabled Poppy to glide down without fear of skidding. Doing that now, she was at the side of the pickup when it stopped.

Micah was out in an instant. He was tall and solid. His dark hair was thick and worn longer than even the country norm. He wore faded jeans, work boots, and a plaid wool jacket that flapped open as he loped around to the passenger's side and lifted both girls out. Each wore brightly colored parkas and carried small backpacks.

"There's lunch in the packs," he told Poppy. "Heather made sandwiches last night. She always does it the night before. . . ." His voice trailed off, and he looked suddenly stricken.

Poppy urged Micah toward the road with a hitch of her chin. "You go on. Get this straightened out." She took the backpack that Missy was already passing to her as the older child moved behind the wheelchair to push. Then she held out an arm to Star.

"I appreciate this," Micah murmured.

"They're okay," Poppy assured him. He looked at them a second longer before returning to the truck. Poppy had Star on her lap by the time the truck was gone. "Did you have breakfast?" she asked.

"We were gonna; then we didn't have time," Missy answered.

"Daddy forgot," Star said.

"Daddy has lots on his mind," Poppy said, "but I have only you." She tightened her arm around Star as they rode up the ramp, entered the house, and headed straight for the kitchen. Everything in it was lower and more accessible than in a standard kitchen.

Poppy was dying to know more about Heather, but she acted as if nothing were unusual as she popped waffles into the toaster. As she buttered them and doused them with syrup from the maple crop Micah had produced the spring before, she chatted with the girls about school, about snow, about upcoming Ice Days. Missy chatted back. Star remained quiet, close by Poppy's side.

"Doin' okay?" Poppy softly asked the little one from time to time, always getting a nod in return, albeit a solemn one. It didn't take a genius to know that the child was worried about Heather.

She'll be fine, Poppy wanted to say. She'll be back. This is all a mistake. Your dad will take care of everything.

But she didn't say a thing, because she didn't *know* a thing. And that irked her. She prided herself on being the pulse of Lake Henry, but she hadn't seen this one coming. She wondered if anyone had.

The more she wondered, the more annoyed she grew. She was adamant in believing that Heather was innocent of what they said. But someone had fingered her. With anyone else, Poppy might have wondered if an ornery Lake Henryite had resented her easy acceptance by the others, but this was Heather. *Everyone* liked Heather.

Poppy particularly doubted that the betrayal had been internal, because there had been so many opportunities for others. Three months ago Lake Henry had been the center of a news event that had focused on Poppy's own sister, Lily, and the media had been all over town. Poppy would put money on the fact that someone from that faction was responsible for this sudden upheaval.

But she couldn't say that to the girls. So after breakfast she helped them back into their parkas and pulled on her own. Outside, she let them ride the lift with her up into the poppy-red Blazer, which had been adapted for her needs. Once the three of them were inside, she made sure the girls were belted in, drove them to school, and gave them big hugs before sending them off.

The instant they disappeared inside, she was on her cell phone calling John Kipling, who was married to Lily and was also the editor of the local newspaper. Since no one answered the phone at their home, Poppy guessed that John was either having breakfast at Charlie's Café or was already at work.

She passed Charlie's first. Snow capped the red clapboards of the general store and adjacent café. She waved to the three men chatting out front, but she saw no sign of John's Tahoe. Less than a minute later she spotted it at the newspaper office, which was housed in a yellow Victorian near the edge of the lake.

Had it been summer, she might have pulled in and talked with John face to face. But this was winter, and winter made maneuvering in and out of the Blazer over icy paths harder to do. So she simply punched in the *Lake News* number as she drove past.

"Kipling here," John answered in a distracted voice.

"It's Poppy," she said. "Do you know what's going on?"

"Hey, sweetie." His voice lightened. "No. What's going on?"

"Heather," Poppy announced, letting loose with her disgust at the situation. She gave him the basics, then said, "I'm wondering how something like this could happen, because Heather is *the* last person I'd accuse of anything, much less false identity and murder. But someone did, and I'm thinking about who the canary could be. No one in town would snitch on Heather. Everyone here loves her. It has to be one of the bozos who was in town last fall during that whole mess that gave Lily her unwanted fifteen minutes of fame—"

John broke in. "Hold on. What happened to Heather?"

"She was arrested by the FBI. I don't know much more. Micah went to go get Cassie. They were going off after the feds. The feds go to federal court, and the nearest federal court is in Concord."

Poppy drove on at full speed. "Federal court." She tried out the words. "Heather in federal court. Doesn't work for me."

"That's because you assume she's innocent."

"Well, don't you? Heather is totally honest. People trust her. Ask Charlie. It took him less than a year to get Heather out of the kitchen and into managing the restaurant. She's the one he leaves in charge when he and Annette go away with the kids—and technically, she isn't even working for him anymore!"

"Poppy, you're preaching to the choir. I agree with you."

"Can you find out who pointed the finger? You're an investigative reporter. Being nosy is what you do best."

"First let's concentrate on what's happening in Concord. Let me make some calls. I'll get back to you when I hear something."

Poppy ended the call. Seconds later she passed the stone

wall that marked the entrance to the Blake Orchards, her mother's pride and joy. If she turned in and drove a half-mile along the gravel road, she would reach her mother's house and, a bit farther on, the cider house. Both were closed up for the winter.

Instead, she turned onto her own road, following it down to the lake. At the house, she quickly maneuvered her chair out of the Blazer and rolled inside to the console that held dozens of buttons. She was anxious for news. John wouldn't have called back so soon, but what she really wanted was a message from Micah.

Even slouched against the wall, Micah was taller than everyone else in the courthouse lobby. Cassie had told him to wait here, so he waited, his fists deep in the pockets of his jacket.

After what seemed like an eternity, Cassie strode down the hall from a room at the end. She was a standout in wool slacks and a blazer and a headful of curly blond hair, but the pickup of Micah's pulse had nothing to do with her good looks. With Heather on his mind, he straightened. When she reached him, Cassie indicated that he should follow her. Down another hall, she knocked quietly on a door, then turned the knob. Micah expected to find Heather inside, but there was only a desk and a pair of battered metal chairs.

"Where is she?" he asked.

"Apparently, still on her way," Cassie said. "There'll be a hearing in a little while. It isn't an indictment, per se, just a hearing in front of a magistrate. Heather won't have to say anything—" She broke off when the door opened again.

Micah's insides lurched. Heather was there with a guard, who gestured her forward. She looked ghostly pale and terrified.

Micah crossed the floor, pulled her into his arms, and pressed her face to his chest as the guard stepped out into the hall and closed the door. Micah held her tightly for another minute, then lowered his mouth to her ear. "Where'd this come from?"

She lifted a shoulder in a muted shrug.

"Have you ever heard of that other woman?"

Heather started to cry. Micah didn't know if that meant she had or she hadn't, but he looked at Cassie in desperation. "She isn't that person. What do we do?"

Cassie came closer. She touched Heather's shoulder, the gesture of a friend. "I need to ask this, honey, because I wouldn't be doing my job as a lawyer if I didn't," she said. "Are you Lisa Matlock?"

Heather's eyes were wet. "I'm Heather Malone."

"There," Micah said, annoyed. "You have it. What now?"

Cassie continued to study Heather's face. After what felt to Micah like an unnecessarily long time, she exhaled. "Now we fight."

Poppy had no calls to take for a while, which was typical of a Lake Henry morning in winter. Cold days tended to keep people at home. They were answering their own phones, reading the paper, or cleaning up breakfast in the easygoing way that Lake Henryites had.

She built a fire in the stone hearth, made a pot of coffee, and sat back with a steaming mug of it to look at the lake, all the while wondering where Heather was. Poppy had friends she'd known longer than Heather, but Heather was the one she liked best. She felt closest to Heather, had from the first time they met. Poppy had been a sophomore at the state university, and Heather, who spent her workweek inside at Charlie's Café, loved the outdoors. Each weekend a group of them went mountain climbing. Thinking back, Poppy realized that she had done most of the talking. Heather was a good listener, and Poppy, who felt constrained by the town in general and her family in particular, had needed to vent. Then Poppy's accident happened, and through the nightmare of recovery Heather had been there for her. She didn't dole out pity or offer patronizing words of solace. Her attitude was to accept what had happened and move on. That quiet approach had been a relief.

Poppy was thinking about that quietness—about listening rather than talking, and whether there had been a reason for it that went beyond Heather's basic nature—when the light for her private line blinked and John's number appeared on the phone bank. She put on her headset and punched in the blinking button. "Any luck?"

"She's at the federal courthouse in Concord. A hearing's going on now. Turns out the guy Lisa Matlock allegedly killed was the son of a United States Senator from California. He got his party's vice presidential nomination three weeks after his son's death, in part thanks to the sympathy vote. The ticket lost, and DiCenza didn't run for the Senate again, but he's still a force in the state."

"And you picture our Heather as the type who would mingle with political movers?" Poppy asked. "I don't. She's too private, too shy."

"Hey, I got this from my buddy who covers the courthouse for the *Monitor*. I'm just telling you what he told me. This was a high-profile case at the time. My guess is it'll get lots of attention now. I'm driving down there myself. I'll call you when I get back."

She simply added, "Please," and disconnected the call.

Slipping off the headset, she took up her coffee and tried to imagine Heather in a cell in Concord but couldn't give the image a face that fit. Heather looked too . . . gentle. The scar did that. It was small, not more than half an inch long, and curved gently upward from the corner of her mouth, the eternal optimist's smile.

Another button lit on the console. This time the number was that of Marianne Hersey's bookstore. Putting one end of the headset to her ear, Poppy pressed the button. "Hey."

"What's going on?" Marianne asked. She was one of five women who had dinner at Poppy's every Tuesday. They were good friends who shared news, laughter, and gripes. Heather had been with them the evening before, as she was every week. "I got to work and was sitting down with my coffee, thinking maybe I'd catch an author on the morning talk shows, and suddenly there's breaking news from Concord. Do you know what they're saying about Heather?"

"On television? Oh God. What are they saying?"

"That she deliberately ran down former Senator DiCenza's son, then fled from the scene of the accident and wasn't spotted again until a member of the FBI's cold-case squad got a lead from someone who was here last fall. What do you know?"

"Not as much as you do. I'm going to go watch. I'll call you back." Poppy aimed the remote at the TV and turned on the set. No more than a second or two into channel surfing, she spotted a "Breaking News" banner. A reporter was talking.

"A major break in the investigation of the murder of Robert DiCenza fifteen years ago in Sacramento. DiCenza, who was twenty-five at the time, was run down as he was leaving a fund-raiser for his father, then United States Senator from that state. The car that hit him was driven by eighteen-year-old Lisa Matlock, who, sources say, had threatened him earlier that evening. The FBI alleges that Lisa Matlock has been living in New Hampshire for the last fourteen years under the name Heather Malone. She was apprehended early this morning at her home in Lake Henry and was transported to federal court here in Concord. A hearing has just concluded, during which Ms. Malone's lawyer formally contested the proceedings. That means that she will be fighting extradition. Since extradition is a state issue, she will be transported to the superior court in West Eames for a hearing later today. This is Brian Anderson for Channel Nine in Concord."

Poppy was befuddled. She and her friends didn't spend Tuesday nights talking about the weather. They talked about private, intimate things. She tried to recall stories Heather had told about her childhood but could think of none. Heather was more of a listener.

Marianne bet that someone who was here last fall tipped off the cold-case squad. Someone had seen a face, imagined a similarity, and thrown a wonderful woman's life into limbo. Poppy wanted to know who that person was.

Standing near the large leather sofa that dominated the living room in his Princeton, New Jersey, town house, Griffin Hughes held the phone to his ear. On the other end was Prentiss Hayden, once the most powerful member of the United States Senate, now in his eighties and retired to his farm in Virginia. Griffin was ghost-writing Hayden's biography and had run into a glitch.

"I don't want it mentioned," Hayden insisted.

"But it's part of your story," Griffin argued gently. "No one will think less of you for having had a child out of wedlock. You took full responsibility. You gave that child everything you gave the rest of your children. Do the others know about him?"

"In my family, yes, but the public doesn't. I'm not of your generation, Griffin. We didn't talk about these things in the good old days. We talked about honorable debate and gentlemen's agreements. We were civil men. Why, I remember . . ."

Griffin listened to the memory, but he'd heard it before. Idly he picked up the television remote and clicked on the set. There was a breaking story from Concord, New Hampshire. Careful to offer Hayden a thoughtful "Uh-huh" at appropriate times, he listened to the news with growing interest. Finally he said, "Can I call you back, Senator Hayden? Later today, maybe tomorrow?"

"Well, of course, but I don't want that issue mentioned. I won't be changing my mind."

"We'll talk tomorrow," Griffin said. He clicked off the phone and stared at the television with a morbid fascination. By the time the broadcast ended, he was furious. Stabbing the OFF button, he tossed the remote aside and snatched up the phone. He punched in his brother's cell phone number and paced to the window.

After a single ring his brother's voice came through. "Yo."

"Where are you?" Griffin asked without preamble.

"Right now? Three blocks from work."

Not Lake Henry, then. Washington, D.C. Griffin was grateful for that. "I've been watching TV, this stuff about Heather Malone. I'm trying to figure out where it came from. Tell me it wasn't you."

Randall Hughes, Griffin's senior by two years, sounded pleased with himself. "Damn right it was me. Is this cool, or is this cool!"

"Randy, that day in your office, I was thinking out loud. All I said was I had seen someone who *looked* a little like that picture on your wall. I never said it was her."

"That's right, and I picked it up from there," Randy said with pride. "That's how it happens with cases like this. It's something totally unexpected that points you in the right direction."

"I didn't point you anywhere," Griffin insisted, wanting to erase the whole thing. "All I said was that the picture reminded me of a girl I saw. Did I even say it was in that town?"

"It didn't take a genius to figure it out. You'd just come from there. Every word out of your mouth had to do with that town."

That was because Griffin had come home enamored of Poppy Blake, whom he'd gotten to know in Lake Henry. "You don't understand. These are good people. You can't do this to good people."

"Hey," Randy cautioned. "I don't know what she's like now, but the law's the law. Fifteen years ago that lady took a walk. It's about time the Bureau caught up."

"With the wrong woman!" Griffin cried.

"No way. Even if she'd had plastic surgery and had that little scar removed, we have her on the handwriting sample. I still can't believe it. I mean, I'm up there a couple weeks ago, and she's working at the library. I ask for a book; she doesn't have it. I ask if she'll write down the name of the nearest bookstore, and bingo! Matched right up to the writing sample we took from her high school files. We have her," he said with smoldering glee. "We have her cold."

"I'd never have said a thing to you if I'd known you'd do this."

Randy sounded wounded. "What's it to you, anyway? You haven't been there in over a month. You lost interest."

It might have looked that way to Randy, but Griffin hadn't lost interest in Poppy. Not by a long shot. He had been intrigued since the first time he'd called Lake Henry four months ago wanting to do a story on her sister Lily, and Poppy had answered the police chief's phone. Spunk. That was what he'd sensed in her. She'd shown spunk.

Then Griffin had felt something melt inside when he had seen her for the first time in that wheelchair. The thing was lightweight, state of the art—and turquoise. That alone was as much of a statement of who she was as her short dark hair. He'd had to cajole her before she agreed to let him take her to dinner, but they'd had an incredible time—had talked a steady stream for three hours.

At least he thought they'd had an incredible time. But when he tried to arrange for a follow-up, she resisted. He knew what she was thinking. She had blurted it out in the very first words she'd said to him face to face. *I can't run. I can't ski. I can't dance. I can't drive a car unless it's been specially adapted. I can't even stand in the shower.*

He understood that she needed time, so he had given her that. He had dropped by later on the pretense of just passing through town, staying no more than a few hours, and every few weeks he sent her a postcard from wherever he was. But he hadn't called in a month. That didn't mean he had been idle. He had gone to extremes to learn everything he could about Poppy.

One thing he had known from the start was that she and Heather Malone were best friends. Griffin was certain—beyond any reasonable doubt—that if Poppy found out that he was the one who had tipped off the cold-case squad, she would never talk to him again.

So he said to Randy now, "If you ever—*ever*—tell anyone that you got the lead on this case from me, you're a goner."

"Whoa. That's a threat."

"Coming from your brother, it sure is."

"Hey," Randy said in a way that spelled blow-off, "I'm driving into the garage under my building. No reception here. Talk later."

The phone went dead. Not that Griffin had more to say. He was thinking that Poppy would never have a friend who was a killer.

After his brother hung up on him, he turned on the television again and watched another update on the case. Several minutes into the broadcast the anchor introduced Randall Hughes, the FBI agent who had cracked the case. Griffin was horrified to see his brother, live on the screen, admit that he had received an anonymous tip from a member of the press corps who had been in Lake Henry last fall, which had then led to the apprehension of Heather Malone.

After the interview was over, Griffin turned off the TV and tried to gauge the damage. Hughes was a common enough name. If Poppy had been watching now, she might not make the connection.

Wishful thinking, he thought sourly. Randy's hair was a deep auburn that could translate into brown in many lights, but there was the jaw they had in common. Put the name with the jaw and add the timing of Griffin's visits, and Poppy would know. A fast phone call would tell him one way or the other.

But he didn't want to find out what Poppy did or didn't know in a phone call. Far better to drive up and press his case in person.

Poppy missed the interview with Randall Hughes. She didn't hear the name, didn't see the face, because she was working. By late morning nearly all her phone lines had lit up. Some of the calls were from townsfolk wanting to confirm what had happened; others were from the media, and Poppy knew all the right words to say. The challenge with those calls came in remaining patient and polite.

Hardest of all, though, were calls like the one from Poppy's sister Rose, because they involved speculation, and speculation raised issues for which there weren't any answers.

"What if they keep her in jail? What will Micah do?" Rose asked.

"They won't," Poppy replied. "She hasn't done anything."

Rose persisted. "Do you think Micah's worried?"

"Of course he's worried. He loves Heather."

"Forget love. Who'll help with sugaring?"

Poppy's stomach began to knot. It often did that when she talked with Rose, who was an alarmist of the first order. Rose was the youngest of the three sisters—the Blake Blooms, as they were known in town. Lily was the firstborn, typically introspective, sensitive, and focused. Poppy was the rebel, far more easygoing than the other two. And Rose? Rose was a clone of their mother, Maida, which meant that she saw the dark side of every issue.

"Why are you fixated on this? Heather will be out," Poppy said.

"I'm fixated on it," Rose returned, "because Heather got all sorts of business ideas from Art"—Rose's husband, Art Winslow—"that she's put to good use. New evaporator, new logo, new accounts. So here's Micah, who's grown the business, thinking Heather would help, and suddenly she isn't there. The weatherman's forecasting sun. If the days start to warm, the sap could be flowing in two weeks. The timing is terrible. How did it happen?"

"I don't know," Poppy said, ending the call and proceeding to worry about all the points Rose had raised.

Griffin drove a gray Porsche. His prized possession, though, was the GPS program he had installed in it the year before. All he had to do was punch in a destination, and a sexy female voice articulated the directions. He called the voice Sage.

Actually, had he been going straight to Lake Henry, he

wouldn't have had to consult Sage at all. He knew the route by heart. Now, though, he was headed for another New Hampshire town, West Eames. Griffin had been monitoring the progress of the case on the radio during the drive north from New Jersey, and he figured that he might just be able to arrive in time to catch the hearing.

His cell phone rang. The return number was one he had dialed an hour before. "Hey, Duncan. Whatcha got?"

Duncan Clayes was a college buddy, currently the reporter for a San Francisco daily. "Lisa Matlock was born and raised in Sacramento," he said, reading his notes. "The mother left when she was five. She was raised by her father. Years before, he'd done time for breaking and entering. They lived pretty much hand to mouth."

"Is the father still alive?"

"No. He died of a heart attack two years after Lisa disappeared. The FBI still doesn't have a clue about the mother."

"Did Lisa have friends?"

"At the time of her disappearance, her father said yes, but none came forward, certainly not to help her. The father claimed that someone reached them first."

"Someone from the DiCenza family?"

"Thereabouts. Rob was a fast one, moving from girl to girl."

"So what was the relationship between Lisa and Rob?"

"Initially the family said there wasn't one. After the murder, though, word leaked out from DiCenza friends that they were sexually involved. The family then changed its story and started talking of extortion. They said Lisa and Rob were arguing that night because Rob had dated Lisa a time or two and was trying to end it, but she was shaking him down for money to keep quiet."

"What would she have had to keep quiet about?" Griffin asked.

"She was the daughter of an ex-con, and she was poor—not the kind of girl his parents wanted—and since the family was headed for big visibility with the vice presidential nomination, she could have held Rob up for money. The family was uptight about its image."

"Your exit will be coming up in a mile," Sage warned. "Please make a left at the end of the ramp."

Griffin moved to the right lane. "Is there more?" he asked Duncan.

"I could find it. Anything in particular or everything in general?"

Griffin didn't know, so he told Duncan, "Everything in general, plus as many photographs of Lisa Matlock as you can get. Overnight them to me care of general delivery at the Lake Henry Post Office. Do this, and we'll be even." Several years before, in the course of writing an in-depth freelance piece, Griffin had come across a valuable tip to an adjacent story. He had given it to Duncan, whose career had taken an upward turn as a result. Duncan had sworn that if he could ever do anything for Griffin, he had only to ask.

Griffin ended the call, coasted down the exit ramp, and turned left. He reached for the phone and punched in the number for Ralph Haskins, an old family friend who was a private investigator. Ralph was aware of the breaking news from New Hampshire, so Griffin didn't have to fill him in when he asked for as much paperwork on Lisa Matlock as Ralph could find. Ralph worked behind the scenes, between the lines, and underground. He had a way of getting information other people couldn't. Ralph was always pleased to hear from a Hughes and was eager to help Griffin now.

Leaving him to it, Griffin ended the call and pressed the radio's SCAN button. Moments later he was listening to the strongest of the local stations. It told him that the hearing was still in progress.

When Griffin arrived in West Eames, he had no trouble finding the courthouse. He parked the Porsche on a side street and reached the courthouse just as the first of those who'd been inside pushed open the large double doors and spilled out. They looked angry—not a good sign to someone praying the whole thing would be dismissed.

Griffin looked around for a familiar face and was relieved to spot Poppy's brother-in-law, John Kipling, with his brown hair and close-cropped beard, coming out of the courthouse. Fighting his way up the stairs against the crowd, Griffin extended a hand. He was thankful when it was met with goodwill. "What happened in there?"

John led him back down the steps. "She's being held without bail for thirty days. Cassie argued that she's been a model citizen, but she didn't have a prayer of winning. Lisa Matlock went underground fifteen years ago. Odds say she'd do it again in a heartbeat."

"You're assuming the woman in there is Lisa."

"Not me," John cautioned. "The judge, the prosecutor, the FBI. *And* the DiCenzas. Charlie DiCenza still has clout. Word has it that he was brought into the loop long before anyone up here was, and he has been making calls. He wants his son's murderer caught and punished. There was no way Heather was being released."

Griffin heard the pain in John's voice. "Cassie'll get her out."

John started down the sidewalk. "Yeah, but do you know what it'll take to do that? Only part of it's the thirty days of

Heather's life, and of Micah's and Missy's and Star's. The other part's the money. Court costs alone will be huge."

"She's innocent," Griffin insisted.

"Well, it'll cost her to prove it. I don't know how they're going to do it. Micah doesn't have that kind of money." John stopped and eyed Griffin strangely. "What are you doing here?"

Griffin stopped alongside him. "I was heading for Lake Henry and got sidetracked."

"Where've you been? Last time we talked, you were interested in Poppy. Disappearing for weeks doesn't say much for that." He set off again.

Griffin kept pace. "She hasn't exactly been encouraging."

"You knew she had issues. Does she know you're coming now?"

"No. I thought I'd surprise her."

"Poppy doesn't like surprises." John stopped at a Tahoe with LAKE NEWS written on the door. "Why now? If you're thinking of writing about Heather, think again. Know how Poppy feels about people who make money off the bad luck of others?"

"I sure do," Griffin said. "I'm not writing about Heather. I'm in the middle of something else, but I have been talking to my contacts about her. Hell, if I can come up with something that'll help . . ."

"Why would you do that?"

"Because I think Heather's being railroaded."

"You think she's innocent? Because she's Poppy's friend?"

"In part."

John stared at him. "Keep going. Poppy'll want to know the rest."

Griffin felt a sinking inside. John knew, then. He had seen the interview with Randy and had put two and two together.

So Griffin admitted, "It wasn't deliberate. When I remarked about that picture on my brother's wall, the last thing I expected was that Randy'd come snooping up here."

John's stare grew vaguely blank before turning into a puzzled frown. "Randall Hughes. Oh God, I'm slow."

It was a minute before Griffin realized what he'd done. With a frustrated sound he hung his head. "Guess I'm slower than you."

John looked angry. "You led them here."

"No, I remarked on a similarity. Randy took it from there."

"Poppy figured it was someone who was here in the fall. She won't be happy it was you. Are you going to tell her?" John asked.

"Probably. I'm not good at keeping things in. On the other hand, if one of my people comes up with something that proves Heather wasn't Lisa, I'll be in the clear. Don't you think?"

John looked at him a minute longer, then shook his head and unlocked the car. "What a mess," he mumbled as he slid inside.

Griffin caught the door before it could close. "I need a place to stay. Will anyone in town rent me a room?" The nearest inn was a fifty-minute drive from Lake Henry. He didn't want to be that far away. If he was to be of help, he needed to hang out in the general store and pick up gossip at the post office.

"The town's going to shut out the press," John said.

"I'm not the press. I'm Poppy's friend."

He glared at Griffin. "That's worse. Know how protective Lake Henry is of Poppy? She's special. Very special. She might be rosy and upbeat, but her life is no cakewalk."

"I know that," Griffin said, and he did.

John started up the Tahoe. "Charlie Owens owns the general

store. His brother moved away a dozen years ago, but he left a place here that needs checking all winter. If you want to earn brownie points with Charlie—and brownie points with Charlie can take you a long way in this town—you could stay right there and do the checking for him." He gave Griffin a guarded once-over. "Nah. Maybe you couldn't. The place is tough. Middle of winter."

"I can handle tough," Griffin said. He had hiked a good part of the Appalachian Trail and was no stranger to rustic accommodations. Wasn't he already wearing insulated hiking boots?

"Little Bear's an island. It's a quarter mile out," John warned.

"How do you get there in winter?"

"Walk or drive. It'd be easy if you had a truck. The Porsche?" John had drooled over it the last time Griffin had been in town. "I don't think so." He began closing the door, but Griffin held it firm.

"I'll rent a truck. I was planning to once I got here anyway."

John brightened. "Well, there's an idea. My cousin Buck's looking to sell his. You could pay him twice what he's asking and win over a whole other side of town."

"Done," Griffin decided. "Where do I go?"

John's cousin Buck lived on the Ridge, which was Lake Henry's version of the wrong side of the tracks. Given that the Porsche wouldn't go over well there, John suggested that Griffin stash it in a boat shed at the local marina for the duration of his stay. That put Griffin in John's car for the ride to the Ridge.

When Poppy passed John's Tahoe in the center of town, though, she was too preoccupied to look twice. Micah had called and asked if she would pick up the girls at school.

As soon as Poppy pulled up at the school, she got out of the Blazer and found a spot on the sidewalk where the girls would see her. She wasn't the only one there, but she was the only one foolish enough to be out in the cold. Other parents waited in the warmth of their trucks. When Missy and Star emerged from the school, they set off at a run toward the parents' vehicles, but when they caught sight of Poppy, they stopped cold. Poppy wasn't Heather.

The questions started the instant Missy reached Poppy's side. "Where's Heather?"

Poppy held Missy's unzipped parka closed with one hand while she opened the other arm to Star. "She's in West Eames."

"Why's she there?" Missy asked.

How much to say? "There are things she has to do there. So I was thinking we could go home and make maple cookies."

"Whose home?" Missy asked wisely.

"Yours," Poppy said.

Missy sighed. "Is Heather gonna be back for dinner?"

"I . . . Actually, I don't think so."

"When is she gonna be back?"

Ten days? Twenty days? Thirty days? How in the world do you explain this to a child? Poppy was starting to tremble. "Soon, I hope, but I'm real cold, Missy. Another minute and my wheels are gonna freeze. Let's get in the car."

As soon as she and the girls were in the Blazer, Poppy headed out. She put her blinker on and waited to turn off the schoolhouse road onto the one that led through the center of town. She had barely made the turn when she felt a hand on her shoulder. Star was there, saying in a small voice, "Did Momma go away?"

"No, honey, she's just over in West Eames."

"Is she gone for good?"

Put your seat belt on, Poppy wanted to say, but Star seemed

so frightened that Poppy couldn't make herself say it. Instead, driving with greater care, she tipped her head and touched her cheek to the child's hand. "She is not gone for good."

"What if she never comes back?"

"She'll be back. She loves you."

It was a minute before Star spoke again, and then it was more an aching sigh than anything else. "I want Momma."

Poppy had never felt so helpless in her life. "I know you do, baby. I know you do."

Now in Buck Kipling's truck, Griffin didn't have time to spare. He had to stop at Charlie's for instructions and supplies, then drive around to the far end of the lake. He figured he had less than two hours to get to Little Bear, open the place up, and get the woodstove going and the electricity on before darkness set in.

The general store was packed with people coming in from West Eames. Grateful that no one paid him much heed, Griffin found Charlie at the cash register. Quickly he explained what he wanted to do. Charlie agreed, albeit with more caution than warmth.

"What do I need to know?" Griffin asked.

Charlie considered that for a minute. "Wood's in a pile on the porch. If you need to chip a little at the pipes for water, use the chisel inside the door. Electricity, just throw the switch."

It all sounded easy enough to Griffin, who stayed only long enough to buy coffee, bread, eggs, cheese, canned soup, and several gallon jugs of water. Figuring that he would need something to help start the fire, he topped off the three large shopping bags with the various newspapers that were for sale. He went back out to Buck's truck and stowed the food in the cab. Then he was on his way.

Heading out of town on the road that circled the lake, Griffin followed John's directions. Little Bear Road was clearly marked. *Drive all the way down,* John had instructed, *out onto the lake.*

Onto the lake? Griffin had asked skeptically. *Can I do that?*

Sure, John had replied. *There's trucks out to bob-houses all the time. No one's fallen in yet this year.*

Griffin set his qualms aside, particularly when he saw that Little Bear Road was plowed. He turned onto the road. When the lake came into view, he smiled. Seconds later his smile faded when the plowed portion of the road ended and the truck got stuck. All four tires were in snow nearly to their upper rims, which Griffin discovered when he climbed out of the cab and sank in well above his hiking boots. Not wanting to waste time, with the lowering sun, Griffin studied Little Bear Island. A *quarter mile out,* John had said. It didn't look far. Griffin figured he could cover the distance easily enough on foot. Putting his overnight bag on one shoulder and his laptop bag on the other, he took a shopping bag in each arm and set off.

When Griffin rounded the island and saw the cabin, he felt a surge of pleasure. It was made of logs, charming in its rusticity. Firewood was piled immediately to its left, under a porch overhang. He waded up to the front door and tried to open it. When it resisted, he set the bags down and put all his strength into the push. Finally the door gave way. He whisked the bags inside and closed the door.

Darkness. Cold. Mustiness.

Electricity, Charlie had said cryptically. *Just throw the switch.*

Griffin pushed back the little cafe curtains that hung on the windows. He spotted a switch on the wall, threw it, got nothing. He tried another switch and another, finally realizing that there had to be a master switch. Intent on calling Charlie, he pulled his cell phone from his pocket, only to find that he was in a no-service zone.

Heading for the kitchen, he opened one cabinet after the other until he found candles, a lantern, and matches. In no time he had the lantern lit, but the relief was small. A woodstove sat inside the fireplace, looking as dark as the cabin and twice as cold.

He went outside to the woodpile. He whacked several pieces together to free them of errant snow and ice and carried as much inside as he could. Making tight rolls of the newspapers he had bought, he put them inside the stove, placed wood over them, and struck a match. He didn't breathe freely until the logs burst into flame. Then he set off to get the rest of his gear from the truck.

Chapter Three

Poppy was worried. The oven had long since cooled, the smell of maple sugar cookies had begun to fade, and the girls would be wanting supper, which, taken alone, was no problem. She would happily make them supper. But they wanted Micah.

She tried reading to them, but they were distracted. She tried to interest them in the dollhouse village in the spare room, but they were quickly bored with that, too. Now, silent and serious, they were watching television.

Poppy had barely heard the sound of Micah's truck, when the girls were up and out the door. She hung back, waiting until Micah shooed them inside again. His face was ashen and his eyes so dark that Poppy felt a jolt. She hadn't seen those eyes so dark in years. The light Heather had put there was gone.

The girls stood inside the door, watching their father and waiting.

Micah simply shook his head and set off for the kitchen.

• • •

By the time Griffin returned to the cabin, he was colder than ever. He wanted heat, but the cabin had been so cold for so long that the warmth of the woodstove was slow in spreading.

He fought with frozen fingers to get his boots off, then pulled on dry socks and a dry pair of jeans. Using the lantern for light, he searched the cabin again. This time he found an oil lamp and a tin of kerosene. With that lit, he went into the bathroom. There was no water in the toilet. He pulled the flush knob. Nothing happened. Same thing when he tried to run water in the sink. Nothing. *If you need to chip a little at the pipes for water, use the chisel inside the door,* Charlie had said. It was there as advised, near an axe and shovel. Griffin picked it up and looked around. Chip at the pipes? What pipes?

It occurred to him then that he'd been set up. If John hadn't known the pitfalls of the cabin on Little Bear Island, Charlie surely did. They wanted him to fail.

Well, he wasn't about to do that. Dropping the chisel by the door, he pushed his feet back into his wet hiking boots and went outside and relieved himself in the woods. He went back inside, where the woodstove had started to warm the area closest to it. Thinking that this was a good sign, he pulled an iron saucepan from the kitchen cabinet and set about heating soup on the woodstove.

The soup was barely hot when he realized that the small scratching sounds he heard weren't coming from the pot.

Sitting at the phone bank later that evening, Poppy received a call from Mary Joan Sweet, president of the local garden club. She claimed to have seen Griffin Hughes driving Buck Kipling's old truck through town. Since Mary Joan was known to be nearsighted, Poppy could comfortably discount her claim. Leila Higgins, on the other hand, was a credible source.

She called Poppy to report seeing Griffin in the general store, which was easy enough to prove. Poppy called Charlie.

"Yup," Charlie confirmed, "he's in town. He's staying at my brother's place on Little Bear."

Poppy didn't hear the last for grappling with the first. "Why's he here?"

"He's chasing after you," Charlie teased, but she didn't hear the teasing either.

"He must be chasing after Heather. He's a writer. He'll use us."

"He says he's working on something else, but if he's snooping, I'd rather he be under my thumb so I can keep an eye on him. Besides, his being on Little Bear sure is a help to me. I wasn't looking forward to traipsing out there to check on the place."

At last the words registered in Poppy's mind. "Griffin's on Little Bear? But the place must be frozen solid."

"Yup."

"He won't get water."

"Not this time of year."

She heard his smile, and unable to resist, she said, "You're bad, Charlie," and let slip a small smile of her own.

Red squirrels. Griffin wouldn't have known that if he hadn't followed the scratching sounds to a spot overhead. He pulled out a ceiling tile and caught a pair of them tearing the insulation apart. He replaced the tile as quickly as possible and returned to the spot he'd staked out for himself in front of the woodstove.

Of course, he'd been set up. He figured there might be folks in town that very minute sitting around Charlie's, chuckling at the idea that the city boy was freezing his butt off in the dark, with no running water and no electricity. He told himself he was paying his dues. He told himself he was getting on Charlie's good side.

But having driven for seven hours, then trekking through the snow and cold, he was beat. So he took cushions off the sofa, laid them out near the woodstove, then took blankets from the bedroom. Stretching out on the cushions, he covered himself and let determination ease him to sleep.

Micah couldn't sleep. He tried, but well past midnight he was still wide-awake. The bed was too empty. Needing to do something useful, he went out to the sugarhouse and flipped on the lights. He avoided the woodpile where Heather's knapsack was hidden and instead went through the main room into the newly furnished addition, which still smelled of fresh lumber. This room was part kitchen—with a huge stove, rows of cabinets and shelves, and worktables—and part office, with Heather's computer on a desk nearby.

He studied the pile of papers on the desk and felt the start of panic. The papers were in folders, as neat and orderly as Heather's mind. Micah knew that the folder labeled ART held sketches of the new logo and that the folder labeled VAC held information on the vacuum system they had just installed. The folder labeled EVAP held details on loan payments for the new, larger evaporator that they had bought the season before. Information on all of it was in the computer. Micah was an expert with a chain saw, a drill, and a bit, but he was in over his head when it came to the computer. If Heather didn't get back soon, he'd be in big trouble.

Breaking into a nervous sweat, he returned to the house, but Heather's touch was everywhere there, too. Copper pots hung in the kitchen; half-made dresses for the girls in pretty patterns were folded on the sewing machine. Sitting in the dark bedroom, he felt numb, though certainly not from the cold. The house was plenty warm, thanks to a furnace that spread heat through the rooms.

He hadn't had the furnace when he first met Heather. He had a blower system then that worked off the heat generated by the woodstove. The system had been fine, assuming the woodstove stayed lit. Letting it die out had been a source of contention between Marcy and him. She didn't think it was her job to hang around the house just to keep it going, not when she had a husband who worked nearby. He argued that she was the one in the house. It wasn't like he was asking her to chop down the tree, split the logs, and carry armloads to the hearth. He did that. All he was asking was that she add logs to the stove when the flame got low.

What he really meant, he had realized after she died, was that he didn't see why she had to be out all the time. Having babies hadn't slowed her down. She had a frenetic energy, like a bright light that was never still. He had tried to follow it, but in the end he had failed. He had inherited the sugar bush from his father, and the sap season was short. He had to make the most of every minute, couldn't slack off. Frenetic energy was a luxury he couldn't afford.

That frenetic energy had killed Marcy. No one had said it in as many words, but it was clear as day. She'd been driving too fast on icy roads. Always too fast, too eager, too ready to get somewhere.

Heather was the opposite, with her soft, steady voice, her clear silver eyes, and her common sense. She loved being at home. She loved sugaring. She loved the girls.

A small whisper of sound came from the door. He looked around just as Star slipped into the room. She didn't say anything, simply came around the bed to lean against his thigh. As he stroked her hair, he felt a catch in his throat. He didn't have to ask why she was awake. Her worries might be fewer than his, but many of them were the same: Where's Momma? Why isn't she here? When will she be back?

Feeling as lost as Star, he scooped up the child and held on. Then needing to be alone with his confusion, he carried her back to bed.

Griffin awoke to a hint of daylight coming through the curtains. In the silence, he could still hear the scurry of feet overhead. Giving the squirrels wide berth, he got up and opened the curtains on a world dense with fog. He needed to use the bathroom, but his hiking boots were still damp. He opened them wider and repositioned them near the woodstove, then set a pot of coffee on to perk. Finally, when he couldn't possibly wait any longer, Griffin put on his boots, went outside, and ran straight for the trees.

The relief was well worth the biting cold. When he was done, he caught sight of the lake. The fog had begun to lift, leaving startlingly beautiful tiers of light. When the clouds thinned enough to allow bits of sun to break through, the snow came alive with glitter, but it was what he heard then that made him catch his breath. From somewhere—nowhere—came the haunting call of a loon.

In that instant he wasn't thinking of paying his dues or proving himself. He had always loved the outdoors, and this was the outdoors at its best. He stayed there until his ears stung from the cold.

Back inside, he felt invigorated. He could do this. He could find the switch to turn on the lights. He could get the water running. He could make the cabin work. All he had to do was get the truck out of the snow, and he'd be on his way.

Poppy worked out until her arms and shoulders ached. She focused on her upper body, moving from one part of the weight machine to the other. She pedaled the recumbent bike with her arms, which in turn moved her legs through a range of motion. But she ignored the parallel bars. That piece of equipment had been her physical therapist's idea, not hers. She hadn't wanted it there, didn't see the point. She wasn't walking again. She could accept that.

Finishing up, she showered and answered the phones long enough to know that Micah had taken the girls to school and that Griffin had survived his night on Little Bear. He had shown up at the general store with a bruise on his thumb from whapping logs frozen together, with a purpling slash on his cheek from slipping against the truck when he was shoving birch bark under his tires for traction, and with stories about hearing a loon. The reports said that he was undaunted and had come looking for high winter boots, thermal underwear, and the secret to turning on the lights at the island.

Everyone in town knew that the fuse box was behind a small panel in back of the peanut butter in the kitchen cabinet, that the loons were gone for the winter, and that Buck Kipling kept a tire chain under the seat of his truck. Poppy wondered if anyone had told Griffin that he wouldn't get water running until the pipes were fixed and that they couldn't be fixed until spring. She wondered when he would show up at her place.

Not wanting to be there when he did, she set off in the Blazer the instant Selia McKenzie showed up to man the phones. By ten Poppy was at Cassie's office in town, and within minutes of that, they were off to visit Heather at the county jail in West Eames.

The county jail was a squat brick building behind the courthouse. Poppy's heart pounded in trepidation as she propelled her wheelchair up the well-shoveled ramp. Inside, she and

Cassie were ushered into a small room with a card table and two folding chairs.

A short time later Heather was led in. She wore an orange jumpsuit and looked as if she'd barely slept. Her eyes widened when she saw Poppy, and she hesitated. It took Poppy offering her arms. After a minute Poppy eased her back. "How are you doing?"

"Awful, awful, awful," Heather whispered, and started to cry. When she tried to hide her face, Poppy hugged her again.

Gently Cassie asked, "Are you all right here?"

Heather pulled back and nodded as she blotted her eyes with the heel of her hands. Rather than taking a seat at the table, she backed up to the wall. "Where's Micah?" she asked in a thin voice.

"He'll be here this afternoon," Cassie replied. "He wanted to come with us now, but I asked him not to. I thought you might feel freer without him here. If we're going to prove that you're Heather Malone, we need to talk about where you were before you came to Lake Henry. I need leads, Heather. Help me, please."

Heather took in a slow breath. Exhaling, she put a hand over her mouth. She looked as if she were going to be sick.

"What is it? What happened?" Poppy asked.

Heather's eyes welled again, but she said nothing.

"It doesn't matter what it is," Poppy tried. "It won't change how we feel about you. That's what being friends is about."

Eyes filled with pain, Heather asked, "How are Missy and Star?"

Feeling rebuffed, Poppy said a less gentle "They're terrible. They're sure that you're gone for good, just like Marcy."

Heather drew in a shaky breath but made no reply.

In the ensuing silence Cassie rose abruptly. "This is not fair to them, Heather. And it's not fair to us. We're your friends, and we love you, but that doesn't take us far in a court of law. We need facts. We need hard facts documenting who you are—like where you were born, where you grew up, where you went to school."

Heather frowned and murmured, "We had no money."

"Public schools are free," Cassie replied. "Where did you go to school?"

When she didn't answer, Poppy asked, "Did you get a driver's license somewhere?"

"I used to baby-sit," Heather said.

"For whom?" Cassie asked.

"They're all long gone. My dad had trouble holding a job. It was worse after my mother left."

Poppy had assumed the woman was dead, since Heather had never mentioned her mother. "Where did she go?" Poppy asked.

"I don't know."

"How old were you when she left?" Cassie asked. When there was no answer, she asked, "So your father raised you? Where?" Still there was no answer. "Talk to us, Heather," she said. "I need to know these things. Give them to me, and I can get you out of here."

Heather huddled into the wall. "I can't."

"It's *that* bad?" Poppy asked.

Heather nodded.

"Worse than being sent back to California and tried for murder?" Cassie asked. "Because that's what'll happen if you don't help me out here."

Heather put her forehead against the concrete wall.

"Talk to us," Cassie pleaded.

Heather took her head only far enough from the wall so that she could press her palms to her temples.

"If you won't talk, people will assume guilt," Cassie said.

Poppy leaned forward. "Help us, Heather. Just give us one person who can vouch for your being you—just one name, one place, one date. . . ." She could have gone on, but it wouldn't have helped. Heather had put her hands over her ears.

"I think we're done," Cassie said in a no-nonsense voice.

"No," Poppy cried, turning to her, but Cassie's face was set.

"We've asked, we've coaxed, we've begged," she said. "I don't know what more we can do. The governor's warrant is due in thirty days. That's how long Heather has to decide if she wants to visit California. At the end of those thirty days she may not have a choice. If that warrant presents evidence that we can't counter, she'll be on the first flight out." She went to the door and rapped hard. It opened, and Heather was retrieved by a guard.

Watching her leave, Poppy felt utterly helpless. The instant the door closed, she turned on Cassie. "What you said was cruel."

Cassie sighed. "What it was, was blunt. Gentle coaxing hasn't helped. I tried that yesterday. Maybe this will."

When Poppy returned home, she took several calls from townsfolk asking questions she couldn't answer. Then, putting the phone bank on audio, she wheeled to the window and looked out over the lake. Visually it was as clean, crisp, and pure as it had been the day before. Emotionally, however, it felt old today—and not unexpectedly so. Poppy experienced this same shift every year in the middle of February, when she suddenly ached for spring—and she wasn't the only one. Ice Days were held in February to give the townsfolk something to look forward to at the end of a long winter, and after Ice Days came the sap. Sugaring season was about celebrating the first crop of the year. It was about the promise of spring. Poppy craved grass on the ground and buds on the trees. She craved loons.

After a bit she returned to the phones. The occasional call came in, but her heart was elsewhere. She was surprised that Griffin hadn't been there already. Each time she heard the slightest sound that might be a car on the drive, she held her breath.

As she drove through town that afternoon, though, she didn't see the truck, and once she arrived at the school and got the girls into the Blazer, her concern for them pushed thoughts of Griffin away.

"We had a spelling test today," Missy said. "I got five words wrong."

"Five out of how many?" Poppy asked.

"Five out of ten. That's *half*," the child informed her. "I got them wrong because Heather didn't study with me."

"I could've helped you. I'm a good speller."

"Did you get all A's when you were in school?"

"No."

"Why not?"

"I fooled around and didn't pay attention. I didn't learn as much as I could have, and I disturbed kids who *were* paying attention, and I got a reputation for being a problem in class, *and* I disappointed my parents. Fooling around in school is not a good idea."

Missy must not have liked the answer, because when Poppy glanced back again, the child was flopped against the seat, staring at the handle of the door.

"How was your day, Star?" Poppy asked as she drove on through town to Micah's house. When Star didn't answer, she glanced in the rearview mirror. "Star?" Still there was no answer.

And so it went for the next two hours. Poppy asked questions or suggested activities, and the girls either shrugged or were silent. She made maple apples, baking Cortlands in dark amber late-season syrup. The girls handed her whatever she couldn't reach in Heather's kitchen, but other than asking when Micah would be back from West Eames, they didn't initiate conversation.

Then Star went outside—just picked herself up from coloring at the kitchen table, walked through the back hall and out the door.

Poppy watched her in surprise, then wheeled around to follow. "Star, where are you going?" The door clattered shut.

Dusk had fallen. It was dark and cold. Star wore no boots, no jacket, just sneakers, overalls, and a skimpy sweater.

Pulling the back door open, Poppy watched her climb the snow on the hill and fade out of view. "Come back here, Star!" she called.

Star didn't reappear. Poppy had visions of the child getting lost, freezing to death before Micah could find her. And Poppy couldn't do anything to stop it. She couldn't go after her, couldn't trek up that hill when it was bare, much less in the snow.

"Missy, put on your jacket and see where she is!" Poppy said.

"She's okay. She's only going to Heather's tree."

"What's Heather's tree? *Where's* Heather's tree? Go after her, Missy. I *can't*." She grabbed Missy's coat from a low hook and handed it to her. "Boots, too," she said, "and take Star's." The girl filled her arms with the things Poppy handed her and set off.

Poppy found the switch for the back light. She sat at the door and watched Missy trudge up the hill through its beam and fade into the dark. Then she waited. Sitting there helplessly, waiting for them to return, she had never resented her handicap more.

It might have been one minute or five. Poppy didn't know. Then Missy reappeared in the light cast from the back porch. When Poppy saw Star behind, she fought tears of relief. She lost the battle when Star reached her. Snatching the child up, she cried softly against her silky hair. "Don't you ever do that to me again, Star."

"Heather's tree was lonely. I wanted it to know I was here."

"Well, I need to know you're *here*, because I can't go after you." She held the child. "If something happened to you up there, I wouldn't be able to help. I wouldn't be able to help, Star."

I wouldn't be able to help. That thought haunted Poppy as she drove home. She was teary still, feeling utterly incompetent as she turned in at the road to her house. She barreled on toward the lake until her headlights picked out Buck Kipling's old heap—now Griffin Hughes's old heap. At the sight of it she felt a surge of anger.

Passing the truck, she pulled up as close to the house as she could. Furious now, she maneuvered her chair onto the lift and down. There was some solace in the fact that she was on the ramp before Griffin got out of the truck and reached her side.

She barely gave him a glance as she continued on to the house. When he reached to open the door for her, she angrily waved him aside, opened it herself, and wheeled in. She went straight to the bank of phones and yanked off her gloves, jacket, and hat.

Griffin came up and planted himself directly in front of her desk.

Poppy focused on the phone panel. She knew her eyes were red. Her heart was beating crazily in sheer annoyance. He pushed his hands into the pockets of his jeans. She could see that without looking at him, thanks to peripheral vision.

Slowly, defiantly, Poppy raised her eyes. By the time they met Griffin's, she was boiling. *Why are you here? Didn't I make myself clear enough? Why can't you leave me alone?*

She didn't say a word, just glowered. And then he had the gall to say, "You look like you could use a knight in shining armor."

She exploded. "And you're it? I . . . don't . . . think . . . so. Besides, I couldn't get on a horse if my life depended on it." Her eyes filled with tears. "I can't climb hills, I can't snowshoe or ski, I can't dance or run or even walk down Main Street, and I certainly can't take care of kids, which is good reason why I'll never have them."

"Is that what you were crying about?"

"That and a million other little things. I have a right, y'know. My best friend is in jail, her kids are lost without her, her significant other is on the verge of the busiest weeks of the year for his business, and I'm stuck in a wheelchair. If things were different, I'd be helping Micah in the woods, *with* the girls, but the reality is that I can't help *any* of them. Right now I *hate* this chair."

She stared at him, daring him to say something patronizing.

What he said, after a moment's thought, was, "Want a kiss?"

"I do *not* want a kiss!"

He pulled a foil-wrapped candy from his pocket and held it out.

She tried to make like she'd known all along what he meant. "I get them from Charlie's, too, y'know. Kisses are a dime a dozen."

"Actually, a dime for ten," he said. Returning the candy to his pocket, he went to the back of the room. A long sectional sofa faced the fireplace, which sat in a wall of fieldstone. He sank into the sofa. "Turning me off with a show of self-pity won't work," he said. "All of us have moments of self-pity."

"When do yours come?" she asked.

"When I think about how I inadvertently mentioned something to my brother that probably resulted in bringing the FBI here. You might as well know. It was me. My brother is FBI. He's on the cold-case squad. When I left here in October, I went to his office and kept staring at the picture of Lisa that was hanging on his wall. She looked so much like your friend. I'm sorry."

The confession stopped Poppy cold. She hadn't expected it, hadn't suspected Griffin of this. After a minute, feeling utterly deflated, she lowered her head to her folded arms and began to cry. "Oh God," she whispered finally. "It's been a wretched two days."

When Griffin said nothing, she raised her head and dared to meet his gaze. "What? No slick words?"

Not only didn't he come up with any, but those blue eyes of his actually seemed unsure. "I want to go over there and give you a hug, only I don't know if you want that."

"I don't need hugs," she informed him archly.

"Not need. Want, maybe."

There was no "maybe" about it. It had been a long time since Poppy had been held by a man, certainly not in the full way that would have given her the comfort she craved. Her chair was the proverbial third person, always there to remind her of her handicap.

She drew in a ragged breath. "I'm fine." But she couldn't

talk about this. "So. You were the one who told them about Heather."

"No. I just told my brother that someone here reminded me of Lisa. He's a good snoop."

His admission gave Poppy a vague sense of power. "So why are *you* here? If you're looking for me, the me you might have scored with left here twelve years ago, and if you're here looking for a story, I'm not helping you out."

"Turn that around. I was thinking I could help you out."

"Were you." It wasn't a question. She didn't want his help. "That's some bruise on your face, by the way."

A mite gingerly he fingered the purple slash. "There was a struggle before I could convince the truck which of us was in charge." His hand rasped coming down over the stubble on his jaw.

"Your thumb looks awful, too. Who is winning the war?"

"Me. Definitely me. I got the cabin warmed up and the electricity on. I can't get the water going, but I'm working on it."

"Don't bother," she took pleasure in informing him. "The piping is bad. It can't be fixed until spring."

Griffin looked dismayed. "Are you serious?"

"Totally. And another thing. There aren't any loons here this time of year. What you heard was Billy Farraway playing his loon pipe. He's seventy-five years old and spends the winter moving his bobhouse around. If you haven't met Billy yet, just wait. He'll find you."

"A loon pipe? Are you sure? It sounded very real. I was talking at Charlie's about hearing a loon. No one there mentioned Billy."

"They wouldn't." Poppy held his gaze until he got the message.

"Ahh. They were letting me put my foot in it deeper."

She nodded. It struck her that between the bruise on his cheek, the stubble on his jaw, and the rumple of his hair he looked a little worse for the wear, but it was a good worse. More rugged. She liked the way his shoulders looked when he put both arms along the back of the sofa. She also liked the way he smiled.

"Have you seen Heather?" he asked.

"Yes. She's in bad shape. She seems unable to talk about this."

"Is that what upset you just now?"

Poppy thought about the crying jag he'd witnessed. "I was taking care of the girls. The little one, Star, wandered out into the woods, and I couldn't go after her. I was totally panicked. It's been a while since I felt as helpless as that." And then there was Micah, returning all stony from visiting Heather.

"You're good to be staying with them," Griffin said. "I can't believe half the town hasn't volunteered to do it."

"They have, but the girls are mine." She rushed to explain. "I mean, only in a way. Of course, the girls are Heather's." But she had to qualify that, too. "Not legally, but in every other sense."

"Why not legally?" he asked.

"She and Micah aren't married."

"Why not? They've been together . . . how many years?"

"Four. Heather never pushed Micah. She never wanted the girls to think that she was trying to make them forget their mother."

"Did you know the mother?"

"Yes. She died in a car accident when Star was two months old."

He blew out a surprised breath. "Were she and Micah in love?"

"Yes. For a little while, at least," Poppy said. "Marcy grew up here in town, but I think she always wanted something more."

"If she wanted more, why did she marry a local?"

"Probably because Micah's tall, dark, and handsome. It's a cliché, but that's what he is. He's also silent, which means he's a mystery. It takes a lot of work to get to know him, which means that *you* may be able to worm the occasional bit of information from me—like you're doing right now—but you won't get anything from him."

"It's an issue of trust between you and me. You trust me."

"Excuse me?" she said. "I do not."

"Yes, on some deeper level you do. So is Micah approachable? If I went to talk with him, would I be welcome?"

"Not if he knows you caused all this."

"What if he didn't? Could I get him to talk?"

"About the weather, the woods, or the sap? Maybe. Suggest writing about Heather, and he'll cut you down cold."

He sighed. "I can't write about her. I'm doing something else. I'm writing a biography of Prentiss Hayden."

Poppy didn't have to be told who he was. The man was a political legend. "I'm impressed. If that's so, what're you doing here?"

"Obviously not winning *you* over," Griffin said. "Okay. I'm here to ease my guilt. If it hadn't been for me, this wouldn't have happened. But I can help reverse it. I have contacts all over the country."

"From your work?"

"Some from that. Some from my father. He's a corporate lawyer turned CEO. He turns companies around. He's built something of a name for himself."

Poppy knew that Griffin was independently wealthy. He had told her that in the fall. Now something rang a bell. "Not Piper Hughes."

"Yes. Piper Hughes." Griffin picked up the remote and flipped on the TV. "Dad's done well, but Granddad was actually the source of the big money. He died and left us each a bundle." He switched channels. "No more breaking news."

"Not about Heather," Poppy said. "Not for twenty-nine days."

"Less than that if we come up with something good. Charges can be dropped."

"Which brings us back to your contacts. Okay, what's the price?"

"A shower."

She rolled her eyes.

"I'm serious," he insisted. "We rich boys are used to hot water. I have none, and now you tell me that I won't be able to get it. Know how grubby I feel? So let's make a deal. One piece of new information—on Heather or Lisa—in exchange for one hot shower."

Appalled, Poppy put a hand on her chest. "I am not letting a strange man use my shower. Go ask someone *else*."

"Yeah, and have them laugh at me? They're already laughing about the loons. I'd put money on the fact that right now someone at Charlie's is taking bets about when I'll cave in and go to the inn."

"If they're not doing it now, they'll do it later. Thursday nights there's music and talk in the Back Room. I'd advise you not to go. After what happened to Heather, this is not a night for a new face."

"And you think they're going to let me in their *showers?* So what do I do? Come on, Poppy. Take pity. Be a sport."

Poppy didn't want him showering at her house. But he did have a point. Besides, being a sport had nothing to do with romance. She could be a sport with Griffin if it meant getting information that would help Heather. "If you think I'm providing towels, think again. And I'm not doing your laundry."

"I'll use the Laundromat. Laundromats are great for picking up information. Even rich boys know that."

"The town won't tell you a thing," she warned.

"We'll see."

Chapter Four

On Friday morning Micah and Cassie headed for the jail. Cassie made it clear that the only reason she was going was to get him the privacy of a lawyer-client meeting room. Five minutes into the visit she found a reason to leave Heather and him alone.

As soon as the door was closed, Micah pulled Heather close.

"Cassie's angry with me," she said in a voice muffled by his shirt.

"So am I. Talk to me, baby." He had never said those words before, never had to. Heather had always known without asking that he liked his eggs over easy, his shirts folded rather than hung, just as he had always known that she loved blue lupines and hot coffee waiting when she reached the kitchen in the morning.

She didn't speak.

"I know there are things," he said into her hair. "I never asked. It never mattered to me. I just wanted you."

He hadn't planned to want her. Four and a half years ago, when Heather had entered his life, he was in mourning for his wife. He had two babies, a business, and no free time. He wasn't supposed to want a woman. And he hadn't wanted Heather when he first met her at Charlie's Café and she had offered to baby-sit while he worked. He liked her. He trusted her. It seemed like a good deal.

At the beginning he came home during the day to check on the girls, but he kept at it long after he knew they were fine. Heather was a quiet, smiling presence in his home. He began to look forward to seeing her. And the change from baby-sitter to lover? It happened after they'd kissed.

Well, they hadn't just kissed. One day when the sap was boiling hard and Micah and a crew were late in the sugar-house, Heather stayed to put the girls to bed. Later, when everyone else had left, she went over to help him clean up. There, with the air sweet and warm and his body hot and heavy, he thanked her with a kiss for her help.

It was the most natural thing in the world. But it wouldn't stop. They kissed, they touched, they undressed. He needed to feel every bit of her. He was so in love he couldn't think of anything else.

He still was that much in love. Now, though, he'd been alone for two nights, and he felt a pain he had never felt when Marcy died.

"They keep asking me what I know," he said. "The FBI even searched the house yesterday. Turned the place upside down. Went through drawers and cabinets. Pulled up the rug and the mattress. They went through the sugarhouse, too." They had even pulled a few logs off the woodpile, which had given him a fright. But they'd soon stopped and moved on. "They didn't get much of anything except the computer. They picked it up and carted it off."

Heather drew back. "But that has all our business files."

"They think there's more in there. Coded messages."

"No, no, no," she cried in outrage. "Micah, it's all to do with the business. They can't take that. You *need* those files."

He snorted. "For what? I can't work that machine."

"Camille can. Call her." Camille Savidge was Heather and Micah's part-time bookkeeper.

"What good'll that do if they have the machine?"

Heather gave a quick toss of her hair and a small, smug smile. "Camille makes backup disks each time she comes to do the books. We thought it was a good thing in case there was ever a fire."

Well, that was something, Micah decided. But it still didn't mean that the business wouldn't fail if Heather wasn't back soon.

"I'm alone, baby," he told her. "I lie in bed alone in the dark, and I'm wondering. I don't know much more'n anyone else. All I know is I wanted to marry you, but you wouldn't. I wanted us to have kids, but you wouldn't. Tell me why."

She wilted with frightening speed. "I have."

Very slowly he shook his head.

She tried, "I couldn't . . . I'm not . . . There's Marcy."

He tried to read something in her eyes, but the sadness there simply set his head spinning. That sadness didn't belong to his Heather. It belonged to someone else. Feeling dislocated, he stepped back. Moments later Cassie returned, and they left.

Micah stewed the whole way home. With each passing mile he became convinced that Heather was hiding something important. It galled him to think that she didn't trust him to say what it was.

Pulling up at the house, he slammed out of the truck and

strode around back. At the sugarhouse, he went straight to the woodpile inside. There he stopped. He stared at the area where the knapsack was hidden, as if he could see it right through the wood. He didn't want to see what was inside. He could call himself a million kinds of fool, but he was still too frightened to open the damn pack.

He went back to the house and snatched up a wool hat, gloves, and a pair of snowshoes. At the woodshed, he stopped for a chain saw, a long-handled axe, and a sled. Then he headed up the hill.

Griffin pulled up behind Micah's truck. When he turned off his engine, he heard the chain saw. The growl was distant but distinct.

He headed up the hill toward the sound and saw an evenly spaced stand of bare maples with snow on their limbs. He had to crest another rise before he finally spotted Micah in the distance. By then Micah had spotted him and killed the saw.

Had Griffin been a timid man, he might have turned and run. Micah Smith was a head taller than he was—the chain saw might have been a toy for the ease with which he held it—and below an orange wool hat his face was threatening and dark.

Griffin tried to look pleasant and nonchalant. When he was within striking distance, he stuck out a hand. "I'm Griffin Hughes."

"I know who you are," Micah said, and turned back to the tree he had downed. With a quick pull he set the chain saw to snarling and went to work on the trunk.

Griffin watched Micah make a clear cut, then move down two feet. The tree trunk was easily twelve inches in diameter and looked healthy enough. He yelled over the sound of the saw, "Was it sick?"

"No," Micah yelled back. He finished another cut and moved on.

"So why'd you chop it down?" Griffin called.

"It was too broad for its own good. The first snow came in October, wet and heavy. The weight was too much. The biggest of the branches broke right off under the weight, took nearly half the crown. A tree won't produce sap without the starch brought in by the leaves. No leaves, no starch, no sap. If I left this one standing, it'd only take sun away from more promising trees in the grid."

Griffin could understand the why of that, but he had dozens of other questions. That said, instinct told him that he was privileged to have gotten as many words from Micah as he had.

Then Griffin spotted the axe Micah had brought with him. Griffin had been barely a teenager when his grandfather had taught him how to split wood at the cabin in Wyoming. Warmed by the memory, he picked up the axe. Then he took the first large log in the line of severed sections and stood it in the snow. He raised the axe high and struck. Like a shot, the log split down the middle.

"All *right*," he crowed, and looked up.

Micah glowered. "Don't sue me if you cut off your toe."

"I won't cut off my toe. I was taught better."

With a disparaging snort Micah revved up the chain saw and turned away.

Feeling invigorated, Griffin split each half of the log again, then started over with the next log and the next.

When Micah was done with the saw, he began loading the split logs onto the sled. "Grab the reins," he instructed, tossing his chin toward the back of the sled, where leather straps trailed from the corners. Griffin caught them up just as Micah began to pull.

It should have been easy at the back end. Micah was the engine. All Griffin had to do was hold on tight enough to prevent a runaway sled. By the time they had gone all the way back down the hill and reached the sugarhouse, though, Griffin's arms were as tired as his thighs. But the work wasn't done. When Micah started tossing wood from the sled to the top of the pile by the sugarhouse wall, Griffin chipped right in. He was flagging badly when Micah straightened and, alert, turned toward the road. "Poppy," he said.

Just when Griffin needed a rush of adrenaline, the sight of the red Blazer brought it. He was setting the last log on the pile when two little girls rounded the corner at a run and made for Micah. They were beautiful children, one slightly taller than the other, both with bright jackets, long dark hair, and big dark eyes. He raised a hand in a wave and said to Micah, "Good workout. Thanks."

He strode off around the house to the front. Poppy was already out of the Blazer and up the ramp at the end of the porch. He reached the door in time to open it for Poppy.

Sending him a wary look, she rolled inside. "Are you bothering Micah?" she asked.

"Nope. Just working up a little sweat." He pulled a candy from his pocket. "Want a kiss?"

She glanced at the candy and seemed about to say something tart, when the back door slammed and from the hall came the sound of running. The smaller of the girls appeared first, then the older.

"Who're you?" the older one asked.

"Griffin," he said, and held out his hand.

"That's Missy," Poppy told him, "and Star just behind."

"Missy." Griffin mimed shaking her hand, then did the same with the younger child. "Star." So Smiths didn't shake hands. "I'm pleased to meet you both," he said. He reached into his pocket, pulled out several candies, and tried a hopeful "Want a kiss?"

"We eat maple sugar candy here," Missy said.

Before Griffin could reply, Star came forward. "I like chocolate," she said in the smallest little voice. "Do these have nuts?"

Griffin scrutinized the wrappers. "Not these." Shifting the kisses to his other hand, he dug back into his pocket. He came up with a single kiss and grinned. "This one does. Want it?"

The child took the candy from his hand, unwrapped it, took a bite, and looked at Griffin. "I like the ones with nuts. If you come again, bring those." She turned and went back into the kitchen. Missy must have gone there, too, because she was nowhere in sight.

"You're playing with fire," Poppy warned. "She is vulnerable."

Griffin arched his brows. "I won't hurt her. She sensed that. Children know right away whether someone coming into the room likes kids or not." He grinned. "Hey. I have something for you."

"I told you. No kisses."

"Nope," he said. As he stood up, he felt the strain in his thighs. A groan escaped before he could push it back.

Poppy smiled. "Oh my. You have a little problem."

"Nothing a hot shower won't fix," Griffin said, and put his mouth to her ear. "I got an overnight pack from California. When do you want it?"

Poppy sat by the hearth in her home, blotting out thoughts of everything but the pack on her lap. She had glanced through it all but was most drawn to the photos. They showed Lisa Matlock in a formal high school graduation shot, a less formal hiking-club shot, and a blowup of her driver's license.

"What do you think?" Griffin asked, looking over her shoulder.

Poppy put the formal graduation shot on top. No resemblance, she wanted to say. These are two distinctly different women. But all she could manage was a discouraged "Amazing."

"They look alike."

"Yes." She glanced up at Griffin. He was still fresh from the shower and looked handsome indeed. "Which doesn't mean it's her," Poppy hastened to say. "People do look alike. There are only so many different eyes, noses, and mouths. Same with hair."

"But even aside from the scar, the smile is the same."

Poppy actually found the eyes more gripping. The graduation shot was in color, and those eyes had the same iridescence as Heather's. She singled one page out from the rest. It was a medical report from the emergency room of a Sacramento hospital, made eight months before Rob DiCenza's death. The cut at the corner of Lisa's mouth wasn't the only thing mentioned. There had been other facial bruises. The doctor noted that though the patient denied it, he suspected domestic abuse.

"Why didn't he pursue it?" Poppy asked.

"He had no legal obligation to do that. He might have pursued something if she'd come in battered time and again, but she didn't. If there were other incidents, she went to a different hospital."

Poppy returned to the graduation photo and searched it for something that didn't match. Lisa's ears were pierced; so were Heather's. Lisa's hair was long, dark, and wavy; so was Heather's. Lisa even had the same uneven edge on her two top front teeth.

"So," Poppy reasoned, "if I were Lisa and I was as smart as

she was, wouldn't I have done something to change my appearance?" She looked up at Griffin. "I mean, it would be just dumb to disappear and then resurface somewhere else looking exactly the same."

"Unless the somewhere else was the last place a lawman would look," he reasoned. "And if she used a new name, new driver's license, new Social Security number, it wouldn't have been so dumb. A few questions on a street corner will tell you who to see where, and a little money closes the deal."

Poppy tried to imagine Heather doing that. It still didn't fit. "So do you have anything else?"

"No. But I'm working on it." He gave a short smile. "Not that I'd give you everything I have at once, not if I want a shower a coupla times a week. You have a great shower, by the way."

"Once you get my shower chair out of the way," Poppy said.

"Light as anything, and worth it. We rich boys are suckers for oversize stalls."

"We paraplegics need them, along with daily meds. I'm thirty-two, and I pop pills every day."

"I've boned up on paraplegia. I know about daily meds. They control muscle spasms. Sorry, angel, but that won't scare me off."

"Okay," Poppy goaded. "What if I told you I have a dark past?"

"You mean the accident?"

For a split second she wondered just what he did know. "Before the accident I was an impossible child. I was bratty and rebellious."

"Poppy, why do I care how you were as a child? People change. Things happen; traumas take place; people adapt. That may be the case with you. It may have been the case with Heather."

"Then you do think she is Lisa?" Poppy asked, pleased to get away from talking about herself. "If so, you're no friend of mine." She pointed toward the door. "Leave. Now."

He grabbed her finger and shook it gently. "I do *not* think she's Lisa. I think she's Heather—"

He didn't finish the sentence. Well, he did. But Poppy heard a final word: *now*. He thought that Heather was Heather . . . *now*.

Poppy opened her mouth and prepared to argue, then closed it again. Her eyes fell to Lisa Matlock's graduation photo. If she hadn't known differently, she would have sworn it was Heather's.

Griffin bolted up from a dead sleep Saturday to the fierce growl of a motor. Convinced that something was about to crash through the cabin wall, he pushed off the blankets and jumped up. Pulling the door open, he peered into a headlight. It was blinding in the predawn dark. The headlight veered to the side, and Griffin made out a snowmobile. He caught sight of something large behind it before the whole thing disappeared around the back of his island. Seconds later the engine went still.

He checked his watch. It was barely six in the morning. Griffin pulled on his clothes, grabbed his parka and a battery-powered lantern that he'd purchased at Charlie's, and went outside. He walked out on the lake in the ruts made by the snowmobile and its trailer.

"How ya doin'?" came the voice of an old man.

Griffin approached. "Billy Farraway, I take it? They said you'd get here sooner or later."

"Sooner's only because of Ice Days. I was on the far side of Elbow Island, and the fishin' was good. But others'll be there this weekend. Don't see the point in sharing my space with whoever chooses to fish. There should be trout here. Got any coffee?"

"Not yet. I can make some," Griffin offered.

"You do that while I set up house. I take it black."

Griffin returned to the cabin, perked a pot of coffee, and carried two steaming mugs outside. By then dawn had spread over the lake. In its pale light he saw that Billy Farraway's house was . . . indeed, a house. It was no more than eight by ten feet and made of wood, with a tin roof and a pipe for exhaust. It sat on a platform, which rested on runners, now immobilized by bricks front and rear.

Griffin opened the door. Inside was a cot piled with down covers, a cushioned chair, and a stove. The old man himself was a vision of bushy gray hair and eyebrows, ruddy hands and cheeks. He was on his knees, feeding the stove from a pile of wood

Griffin handed him a mug. "Are you out here all winter?"

"Just about."

Griffin eyed the woodbin. "That bit of wood won't last long."

"The woodman delivers."

"Who's the woodman?" When Billy pushed the question aside with a negligent wave, Griffin asked, "Where do you live when it isn't winter?"

"I got a camp on the shore. There's a bunch of us old guys."

"You've lived here all your life?"

He nodded. "All my life." The old man looked lost in thought. "Don't know what happened with her, though. I liked her."

"Who?"

"Heather." He shot Griffin an annoyed glance. "Who'd you think I was talking about? Who's *anyone* around here talking about? Doesn't matter if you live on the lake like I do. You hear. You hear lots. Course, they don't ask me what *I* know."

"What do you know?" Griffin asked nonchalantly.

Billy looked at him. "I know that I don't know *you*."

Griffin held up a hand. "I'm safe."

Billy snorted. "I know about sugaring, I'll tell you that. Know how to drill to hit sapwood. Know how to keep the pan from burning. Know just the instant when the boil changes and you got syrup."

"How do you know that?"

He frowned, then scowled. "Achh. Doesn't matter." His brows rose, and his expression brightened. "Want to watch me wet a line?"

During Ice Days, Poppy drove an Arctic Cat. She didn't own it. The local dealership was run by a friend who hoisted her up, strapped her in, and provided helmets for her and her crew. Poppy felt safe in the Cat. It was an all-terrain vehicle with four large deep-treaded tires, an automatic gearshift, and a rear box that could hold three hundred pounds' worth of food, drink, or kids.

Today the rear box contained two dozen large pizzas in insulated bags. They were held in place by bungee cords and Missy and Star, the two girls half hidden under their helmets.

Poppy raised her faceplate and looked back. "You girls okay?" The girls each raised a mittened thumb and grinned.

The grins were what Poppy wanted most. There had been none at all that morning when Micah had dropped them off. "Gotta work," was all Micah said when Poppy opened the door, and she didn't argue. Poppy knew enough about sugaring to understand the pressure he felt. She had grown up with seasonal pressure, albeit with apples rather than sap. She knew what it meant to harvest those apples and get them to market while they were crisp.

Sitting on the Arctic Cat now, Poppy lowered her faceplate. She drove the Cat out onto the lake to the pizza hut that Charlie had set up. When Charlie's two oldest boys had unloaded the boxes, she and the girls explored. They drove around in a slow arc, passing incoming snowmobiles. Farther out, there were car races to watch and, farther still, open patches where ice sailers caught the wind in a stream of vivid colors against the snow.

When they had seen it all, they returned to the town beach. The crowds had arrived. People in snowsuits milled on the lake, their breath white as they talked, their cheeks red. Aware that there was prize money at stake, fishermen mingled around the big board at the fishing derby headquarters, applauding the arrival of new catches as each was weighed, tagged, and hung on display.

Poppy knew that if past years were any indication, there were out-of-staters in the crowd, but the only one she spotted for sure was Griffin. The bright sun brought out the red in his hair, and with only a blue wool headband to keep his ears warm, that hair was a beacon. She refused to look for it, but there it was.

He caught her eye once and waved. She waved back and returned to the conversation at hand. Ice Days were social events. People who had been inside for the worst of the winter months were aching to be outside, aching to see friends, aching to talk. There was incidental gossip—a birth, a death, a divorce. There was talk of the weather. Of course there was talk of Heather, and since Poppy was Heather's closest friend, she was a target for questions.

The first few questions were the least harmful: Why Heather? Why so suddenly? Then came observations that should have been innocent but carried a probing edge: What does Micah know? He has to know more than we do. He's lived with her for four years.

Consternation seemed to be the bottom line: We don't know a thing. She's been one of us for fourteen years, and we're in the dark. How can a person keep so much of herself hidden?

Griffin mingled with the crowd on the lake, trying to be friendly. He asked about the bob-houses that had appeared overnight, asked about bait the fishermen used, asked about the ski races to be held the next day. He wanted to ask about Heather. He was as curious as anyone. But being an outsider, he didn't dare raise the question. He did lean close when he heard the locals talking.

Inevitably, when they caught him at it, they quieted right down.

He wandered off and stood on the packed snow that covered the ice. Poppy was everywhere, tooling around in her four-wheeler. He caught her eye once and waved, and she waved back, but she didn't come over to him. Here in town she was in her element.

In time he grew lonely. By early afternoon he traipsed back to the truck. He had work to do on his biography of Prentiss Hayden. Yet Buck's truck didn't head for Little Bear. It headed for Micah's.

How can a person keep so much of herself hidden?

Poppy didn't remember who asked it. She began to think more than one person had, because she kept hearing the words. Desperate for an escape, fearing that the day would be gone all too soon, she took the girls for a pleasure ride on the lake.

"Hold on," she called back, and accelerated. The Arctic

Cat bucked over a ridge, then hit the lake with a growl and took off.

Turning the large handlebars, Poppy weaved in and out of the bobhouses, exchanging waves with the fishermen. When Missy shouted, "More!" she circled around and repeated the zigzags. The delighted squeals she heard from the rear box warmed her heart.

Settling into the trail left by the snowmobiles, she drove on for a bit until they reached an untouched part of the lake. Unable to resist, she turned the Arctic Cat onto the virgin snow and upped the speed. It was exhilarating. The path was open; the air was clear; the world was pure. For a few minutes her handicap ceased to exist.

Then she felt a flash of memory, a stab of fear. Slowing quickly, she looked back. The girls were fine. At a saner pace she made a large circle and headed back to town.

Poppy focused in on a sheltered spot near the shore. "Oh my!" she exclaimed. "We nearly forgot the face painting." She pulled up close so both girls could scramble out.

"Hi, Aunt Poppy!" came a shout from six-year-old Ruth, her sister Rose's youngest, waiting her turn. The middle daughter, seven-year-old Emma, was right beside her.

Rose separated herself from a group of mothers standing nearby. "I was watching you," she half whispered as she reached Poppy. "I can't believe how fast you were going. It'd be one thing if you were alone. But with the girls?"

"The girls had helmets. And they were belted in."

"It isn't just this," Rose said, rapping a hand against the Arctic Cat. "I know you're Heather's friend, and helping with the girls is a wonderful gesture, what with everything Micah has on his plate. But isn't it taking an awful lot on yourself? I mean, what if there was a problem? What if one of them fell? Could you pick her up?"

Poppy bristled. "Yes, I could pick her up."

"How?"

"The same way anyone else would—in my arms. My arms are strong, Rose. I'll bet they're stronger than yours."

Rose sighed. "They may be, but spills are only the start. You've never been a mother. You don't know what the challenges are."

"Blind women have kids," Poppy argued. "Deaf women have kids. Women with *rock-bottom IQs* have kids. Are you saying I'd be any worse off? But I'm not planning to have kids. I know the risks. All I'm doing here is helping my friends. If you're so worried about Missy and Star, why don't you pitch in, too?" She regretted it the minute she said it, because she knew what was coming.

Sure enough, Rose said, "That's actually a terrific idea. We figured these two would be exhausted after today, so Art is renting a couple of movies, and we're bringing in pizza. I'd love having Missy and Star, too. Do you think Micah would let them come?"

Poppy figured that Micah would be working well into the night and would be glad that they had somewhere to go. Of course, that meant Poppy would spend the evening simmering about what Rose had said, but it couldn't be helped.

Griffin felt a keen sense of satisfaction. Micah hadn't said more than a handful of words all afternoon, but as daylight waned, the main room of the sugarhouse, which was warm and moist and smelled faintly of bleach, was filled with the fruits of their labor. They had washed and triple-rinsed innumerable coils of plastic tubing, many buckets of spiles, and a dozen stainless steel implements. Griffin had no idea what they were for, and he didn't ask. It felt like small talk, for which Micah didn't seem to have the patience.

Now, though, curiosity nagged. While wiping down the long steel sink, Griffin pointed to a large machine. "What's that?"

Micah shot the item a glance. "Reverse osmosis machine. It removes water from the sap before the sap hits the evaporator."

"And that?" Griffin asked, indicating another machine.

"A filter press. As soon as you have syrup, you pour it hot through there. You can't have sugar sand in your syrup—not in top-quality syrup. Lower-quality syrup, lower price."

"How much syrup do you make?" Griffin asked.

"In a good season? Twelve hundred gallons, give or take. The longer the sap runs, the more syrup you make."

"What determines the length of the run?"

"The weather. Sap runs when the nights are below freezing and days are above. All cold or all warm, and the sap won't flow right. Sap can run for six weeks, or it can stop after two."

"You learned the business from your father?"

"And his father. And my uncle." Micah looked at Griffin and came close to smiling. "They were doin' it at a time when you didn't have reverse osmosis machines or filter presses. Hell, they were using *buckets* when I was a boy." He paused, seeming lost in the thought. Then the memory faded. "Of course, they didn't have the acreage I have now. There's no way I could haul buckets in from fifty acres every day. So we use tubing now, and it cuts the work way down. That keeps it a family operation. At least it's supposed to be. I was counting on Heather—" He stopped short.

Griffin remembered the warmth a minute ago. "I wanted to talk to you about that."

Micah shot him a disparaging look. "I was wondering when that'd come."

"I can help. I have contacts. I can get information other people can't."

"What's in it for you?"

Griffin couldn't get himself to talk about guilt. So he said, "Poppy. I like her. I want to help her friends."

"Did she send you here?"

"No. She's protective of you. She's not sure I'm a friend."

"If she isn't sure, why should I be?"

"Because you have my word. And my reason goes beyond Poppy," he added. "I come from a different place. I've been lucky that way—spoiled that way—but I do have these contacts. I use them for stuff that I don't really care about. This I care about. I like Lake Henry. I like the people here. Heather's getting a raw deal."

Micah turned to Griffin, his eyes dark. "What'll it cost me?"

"Nothing. This won't cost me anything, so it won't cost you anything. But the thing is, you're the linchpin here. You're the one who can point me in the right direction."

Micah began snatching up wet cloths from around the room.

"I don't need much," Griffin coaxed. "A birthplace would be great, but if you don't know that, a town, a school, a church?"

"I can't tell you." Arms laden with cloths, he went out the door.

Griffin grabbed their jackets and followed him. "Because you don't know? You've been together four years. She must have mentioned something, must have dropped hints."

"If she did, I didn't get them," Micah muttered as he strode toward the house along the path of packed snow.

"Mail," Griffin tried. "Does she ever get personal mail, a birthday card, a postmark from somewhere strange?"

"No. But I'm not the one who picks up the mail."

"Might she have hidden something?"

"No." He pulled the back door open and went inside.

Griffin followed him in through the kitchen to the adjacent laundry room. "It's not like we need a biography. All we need is one thing to put her in a place other than the one where Lisa Matlock can be proven to be at a given point in time."

Micah stuffed the washer with towels. "I don't have one thing."

"A trip she took," Griffin tried. "A birthday present."

Soap went in. The lid slammed down. The washer went on.

"A relative, any relative," Griffin went on, following him back into the kitchen. "You must know something," he charged, pushing, hoping that the heat of anger might produce a crumb. "She had to be somewhere before she came here."

Micah lost it then. Eyes blazing, he shouted, "If she was, I don't know where! Do you think that makes me feel good?"

A dead silence followed the outburst. Griffin caught the smallest movement in the corner of his eye. Glancing back at the door, he saw Poppy. Her eyes were on Micah. She looked devastated.

Griffin let out a breath. "No, I don't suppose it does," he said quietly. Discouraged, he said, "I've done enough for today, I guess," and let himself out the back door.

Micah came close to opening the knapsack that night. He actually removed it from the woodpile and fingered the buckle. He told himself that there was probably nothing inside. Still, opening the knapsack behind Heather's back seemed like a betrayal.

He even went so far as to ask himself what was the worst thing he could find. The worst was identification papers saying that Heather was Lisa. Coming in a close second, though, was documentation that Heather was married to another man. If Heather was Lisa, he wasn't ready to know. So he put the knapsack back in its groove, piled the wood back to cover it up, and walked away.

Chapter Five

It began to snow in the wee hours of Sunday morning. Feathery and light in the cold air, the snow turned the view from Poppy's bed into frosted candy, but that didn't help her mood. After spending most of the night drifting in and out of a troubled sleep, she awoke feeling weighted down.

She stayed in bed later than usual. When she finally pulled herself up, she showered, put on a green sweat suit, and made a pot of coffee. She turned on the phones, but not a button was blinking. The world of Lake Henry was either sitting in front of a fire and taking its own calls or was over at the mountain, where Ice Days had shifted for ski races, snowboard contests, and toboggan runs.

When the coffee was ready, she wheeled herself to the living-room window, which was where she was when Griffin's truck came down the drive and stopped beside the Blazer. Poppy didn't move. She didn't know how she felt about his coming—couldn't muster anger or even mild annoyance. She suddenly wondered if he'd brought lunch. Hot chili from Charlie's would be nice.

He stomped his feet at the front door, then knocked. She said nothing. He knocked again, then turned the knob, opened the door, and called, "Anyone home?" Spotting her, he smiled. "Oh, hi." He slipped inside and closed the door. "How're you doing?"

"I'm okay," she said. "You're all bundled up."

He toed off his boots, pushing them aside, then pulled off his headband, shaking it free of snow. "It's really coming down."

"They must love it at the mountain. I'm surprised you aren't there."

"I was," he said. He didn't move from the door. "I thought you'd be there, too. You seemed to be having a good time yesterday."

"Yesterday was on the lake. Today's for skiing and all."

"Have you ever tried a sit-ski?"

She felt a twinge of discomfort. "What do you know about those?"

"Only that they're supposed to be fun."

"Ahh. You've talked with people who've used them."

"Actually, yes," he said, and opened his parka several inches. She saw a red waffle-weave shirt and, from the bunching at his middle, guessed he had a fleece in there, too.

"Did you talk with people about sit-skis while you were boning up on my disability?"

He didn't flinch. "I wouldn't call it boning up. I was curious."

So was she. "What do you know about my injury?"

"Only that it's to the lower spine. It's an incomplete injury."

"Which means," she picked up, "that I'm not as bad off as some, that my abdominal muscles function, so I have control of things that some paraplegics don't, that I could probably get myself to walk, though it certainly wouldn't be pretty. Someone here in town blabbed. Who was it? My physical therapist? My masseuse?"

"Whoa. A masseuse here in town? Any good?"

"Griffin."

"Let's not argue. It's just that you looked so pleased yesterday on the Arctic Cat that I was sure you'd be doing something like that on the mountain. Would you toboggan with me?"

"No."

"Go on a snowmobile?"

"No. Why are you harping on this?"

"Because I know that you can do these things, and I want to do them with you."

"I told you I couldn't," Poppy reminded him. "I told you last fall. If you got your hopes up, that's your problem. I look at the positives—all that I *am* comfortable doing. I'm much more fortunate than some, and I'm grateful for that. I'm comfortable with my life."

"Okay," he conceded. "You're right. You did tell me last fall. So maybe it's just that I'm desperate to be with a friend because I'm feeling like a pariah around here. No one would talk to me at the lake yesterday, so today I drove over to Charlie's. The place was next to dead except for this lady. We got to talking, and before I knew it, she was opening her shoulder bag, and out came a cat."

"Ahh." Poppy pictured the scene. "Charlotte Badeau. The cat lady. She takes in strays and tries to find them homes." Poppy had a sudden thought. "You didn't." She studied the bulge of his parka. When he didn't deny it, she felt a wave of absurd affection. "You're a city boy. Do you have any pets—cats, dogs, gerbils?"

"No, but this one's so sweet." He peered inside his coat.

"She's still asleep. Oh"—he caught himself up with an excited whisper—"no, she's waking up." His voice jumped an octave. "Hi, baby."

Poppy saw a tuft of orange fur against that red waffle weave. Excited in spite of herself, she said, "Let me see."

Crossing the room in his stocking feet, he opened his jacket and squatted by Poppy's chair.

The cat was entirely orange. "She's a redhead, like you," Poppy said in delight as she stroked the cat's warm little head. "Look at those closed eyes. She's still sleepy." The head had turned at the sound of her voice, and at her touch the nose began sniffing her hand. Looking closer, Poppy caught her breath. "Oh my."

"Yeah," Griffin confirmed. "How could I say no? Apparently she was born sighted, but then something happened. Whoever had her couldn't deal, so they abandoned her. The cat lady's had her for a couple of months."

Poppy lifted the cat out of his parka and drew her close. "Well, hello," she cooed. The cat sniffed her neck, her ear, her face. "What do you smell? My cologne?" The cat nuzzled Poppy's ear.

"She has good taste," Griffin said so sweetly, so gently that Poppy was left without words. He was handsome, definitely handsome, with his auburn hair, blue eyes, and a shadow on his jaw that said he hadn't shaved since he had been in her shower two days before.

Looking at him now, something caught in Poppy's throat. She was swept back to the first time they'd met, she in her wheelchair, he on foot in the church at the center of town. Prior to that, she had felt a connection between them on the phone, but in person it was stronger—stronger than anything she had ever known.

The cat leaped to the ground.

"Wait!" Poppy cried, and her eyes flew to Griffin. "Catch her."

"No, no. She's okay."

"She doesn't know her way around. She'll hurt herself."

Seeming to draw her head up with pride, the cat straightened and began to walk toward the desk. With startling precision she stopped at the nearest leg, explored it with her nose, rubbed it with her cheek, then moved to the next leg and the next. When the desk had been mapped, she moved with regal grace toward the wall.

Poppy held her breath, fearing that she would hit it head-on. Instead, she stopped and turned to walk its length, as if she'd done it hundreds of times before. Then she proceeded down the hall.

Griffin said a quick "She's looking for a bathroom" and dashed back to the door, pushed his feet into his boots, and raced out.

Poppy started down the hall just as the cat disappeared into the kitchen, and the scene was the same there. The cat explored. She walked, she sniffed, she rubbed. At one point she rose on her hind legs, with her front paws on the cabinets leading to the counter. Poppy picked her up, set her on the granite, and turned on a trickle of water. The cat perfectly positioned her mouth under the trickle.

There was a noise at the front door, then a padding trot down the hall. Griffin appeared, snowflakes still in his hair. He carried cat food, a large plastic pan, and a huge bag of litter.

Poppy took a dish from a drawer, and Griffin filled it with pellets of cat food. He held the bowl under the cat's nose for a split second to get her attention, then set it down in a corner. The cat was there in an instant. Crunching sounds came from the food bowl. When she was done eating, the cat cleaned her face, first with her tongue, then by licking a paw and using that to clean her muzzle.

"So, what's her name?" Poppy asked.

Griffin looked pensive. "I was thinking about that driving over here. Baby seemed a good name then, but now I'm not sure."

"You cannot call this cat Baby. That's an insult, given how courageous she is."

"So what's a courageous name for a girl?"

Poppy thought. "Victoria," she said. "For majesty." With exquisite aim the cat walked straight to Poppy, jumped up onto her lap, and like silk drifting down, settled into a ball. She began to purr.

"And you can't take her to Little Bear," Poppy decided. "She's oriented here now. It would be cruel to uproot her again."

"But she's my cat," Griffin said.

"She can stay here."

"Only if I stay with her for part of the time."

Poppy eyed him suspiciously. "What does 'part of the time' mean?"

Griffin said, "It means absolutely nothing except that I have work to do and you have a huge desk with more than enough space for me to spread out my stuff. You have heat and electricity. You have a bathroom. And cell phone reception. You also have a kind heart. Don't try to deny it. I didn't ask you to take in this cat."

No, he hadn't. But Victoria was warm against Poppy's abdominal muscles. Curled up in Poppy's lap, she was a perfect fit.

"Where's your stuff?" Poppy asked. "Your papers and all?"

"At Little Bear," he replied.

She glanced at her watch. It was nearly noon. "If you were to go back and get what you need, then stop at Charlie's for chili, could you be back by one?"

"Sure. Why?"

"Because if you can, and if you're willing to cover the phones while you work, I could go visit Heather. Think the driving's okay?"

The driving was fine, but then, Poppy was feeling strong. She had chili in her stomach and the comfort of knowing Griffin was at her house working. Nothing wrong with that. He was covering her phones. It was perfect. Besides, she was a pro at driving in snow. She reached West Eames without so much as the hint of a skid.

Poppy hadn't counted on a large room filled with inmates and their guests, or on the alarm that hit her seeing those others, who were so unlike Heather. She managed to grab a free chair and an empty space by the wall.

Heather spotted her immediately, came over, and slipped into the chair. She put her elbows on her knees, leaning close. Poppy did the same, giving them an element of privacy.

"I know," Poppy began. She had seen that quick search of the room and the flicker of disappointment. "I'm not Micah. I'm sorry."

Heather seemed resigned. "I figured he was working, but when they said someone was here, I was hoping . . ."

"He's been washing all weekend. He's planning to lay tubing this week. He wants to be ready when the sap starts to flow."

"I should be there. Has he called Camille about the paperwork?"

"I don't know."

"She knows everything, Poppy. Make him do it. Tell me about Missy and Star."

"They don't understand all this. None of us do. That's why I'm here. Talk to me, honey. Tell me what happened."

Heather's eyes glazed over.

"No, no, no," Poppy said. "Don't *do* that. It doesn't help. When you tune out, you hurt yourself and everyone else. Talk to me."

"Oh, Poppy," Heather whispered. "Did you ever wish you could live your life over—just go back and do things different from how you did them the first time around?"

"All the time. You know that. One ride on a snowmobile—thirty minutes—and everything changed. I'd give anything to do those thirty minutes over again."

"But you can't. All you can do is go on."

"That's what you always said. We both did. But maybe it isn't the only way to go. Whether you're Lisa or not—"

"I'm not Lisa."

"They'll take you back to California and put you on trial. You could be innocent, but unless you give Cassie something to work with, you'll be convicted. So then there won't *be* any going on."

"I'm not Lisa," Heather repeated.

Poppy looked down. She gave Heather's hands a squeeze. "Is that because it would be too painful to be Lisa?"

Heather shot back, "Is it too painful being Poppy?"

"Being the Poppy I was? Yes, it is. She did some things wrong, and that brings pain. There's pain, too, in good stuff that's lost."

"Like?"

"Her spirit. Her daring. Her energy. She was fun. She was also difficult and defiant and foolish, and a lot of that's really hard to think about. But my situation's different from yours. If something happened to me, no one would be the worse for it. I don't have a Micah, and I don't have a Missy or a Star. They *need* you."

With a tiny tremor Heather sat straighter.

"So maybe it comes down to punishment," Poppy said. "You could have married Micah and had more kids, only you didn't. Were you punishing yourself for something that happened before?"

For a minute there were only low murmurs from the rest of the room. Then Heather asked, "Don't *you* do that?"

"Punish myself? How?"

"By limiting what you do. Like with a man. Aren't you curious?"

"Sex? I had plenty of it before the accident. I'm not looking for more." To make her point, Poppy said, "Griffin's back in town."

Heather's eyes went wide. "He is?" As quickly as excitement had flared, it died. "Oh. He wants to write about me."

"No. He says he wants to help. He has contacts none of us have."

Tentatively Heather asked, "Where are Griffin's contacts?"

Poppy felt a glimmer of hope. "All over. He has a network. If there's someone you need to find, or documents or relatives, he's good at this. He has pictures of Lisa. Looking at them is amazing. You can understand why someone made this mistake."

Heather sat very still. Then she opened her mouth and soundlessly formed three words. Before Poppy could react, before she could even wonder if she'd read those words right, Heather was up out of the chair, across the room, and out the door.

• • •

Griffin had fun playing the role of telephone operator. Having been on the other end of the line when he had called for information on Lake Henry and Poppy had blown him off, he did it now to others with flair. Three media calls came, and he was cordial but firm; Lake Henry had nothing to say on the matter of Heather Malone.

He enjoyed the other calls, too. People asked where Poppy was and when she would be back. They asked who he was and whether he was dating Poppy, and he answered in good humor, because the questions weren't one-sided. From the postmaster he learned that Poppy hadn't picked up her mail since Tuesday. From the masseuse he learned that she had a massage every week. He also learned that Poppy hadn't dated anyone special since Perry Walker.

Between calls he phoned Senator Prentiss Hayden. He had been prepared to talk as if he was heavily into the bio. Prentiss nixed that, though, by launching into a spirited "My telephone says this call is from New Hampshire. You're up there, aren't you?"

"Sure am," Griffin said. "Quiet places are great for writing."

"Hah. You're up there for the DiCenza case. Who's the article for this time?"

"There's no article. I just happen to know people here, and it is a good place to write."

"While you snoop around," the Senator said. "Are you learning anything interesting? Give me something to share so I'll sound like I still have an iron or two in the fire."

"I don't have much to share. We're waiting this out just like the rest of the country."

"Everybody's speculating here, and not about nice things. Did you get the information you needed from my army buddies?"

"I did. I've incorporated it into the body of the chapter on the war. I'm still worried about the other issue, though."

"What's it like up there?" Prentiss asked deliberately. "Pretty town?"

"You bet." Another call lit up the board. "I'm going to have to run, Senator. I'll get back to you, okay?"

He took the next call. It was a local one and easily dispatched. When it was done, he called private investigator Ralph Haskins. He answered after a single ring.

"I don't have much to tell you," Ralph said, "or I'd have called you myself. I'm running into stone walls. I don't know whether the Senator's people made a recent round, but I've been talking to people who knew Rob and Lisa fifteen years ago, and they won't say a thing. They claim that they don't remember or that it was too dark to see on the night Rob died, which was what they told the police at the time."

"But I thought there were witnesses saying Lisa threatened Rob."

"I've tracked down three of those, and they all have similar stories. They didn't hear words. They saw anger and pushing. I did find another ER appearance, though. It was in a clinic near Stockton. She used an assumed name and paid in cash, but after the murder, the staff was sure Lisa and that girl were one and the same."

"What made her go to the clinic?"

"A pair of broken ribs."

Griffin swore softly. "Do we know Rob did it?"

"She wasn't seeing anyone else, which brings me to another piece of news. Someone on the local FBI team played college football with Rob. He didn't have much good to say about him. Maybe he has an axe to grind, but he flat out said Rob was rough on girls. He said he'd witnessed one incident where the girl might have been hurt if a group of them from the team hadn't pulled Rob off."

Griffin heard a car approaching the house. He felt a quickening at the thought of Poppy's returning. "Thanks, Ralph."

Griffin disconnected the call at the same time the front door opened, but Poppy didn't wheel through. The woman who slipped in, set down a bag, lowered the hood of her parka, and looked hopefully around was twenty-plus years older than Poppy. Her hair was short, dark, and stylishly cut. Her eyes were gentle and her skin tanned. If ever there was an indication of how handsomely Poppy would age, Maida Blake was it.

Driving home, Poppy took several small skids. She blamed them on the snow, but the bottom line was that she was distracted.

It's no mistake. That was what Heather had mouthed. Poppy had been telling her about Griffin's pictures of Lisa. *You can understand why someone made this mistake*, Poppy had said.

It's no mistake, Heather had mouthed.

Poppy felt stunned. She was disappointed. She was frightened. She was confused. She was hurt. All these years Heather hadn't lied. She simply hadn't told the truth.

Well, hell, Poppy hadn't either. But that didn't mean she wasn't a good person now. If Heather was responsible for Rob DiCenza's death, there must have been justifiable cause.

The only one that came to Poppy's mind was self-defense, and the person she wanted to run it past was Griffin. But when she came down the newly plowed drive to her house, his truck wasn't the only one there. Maida's SUV was parked beside it.

Uneasy on several counts, Poppy pulled up to the house

and maneuvered out of the Blazer. All the while she was wondering what Maida would be saying to Griffin and vice versa. She was barely at the top of the ramp when Maida opened the door and said with a grin, "I'd shout, 'Surprise!' except that isn't my style."

Seeing the grin on her mother's face, Poppy felt pleasure in spite of herself. "You're not here, Mom. You're in Florida."

"Oh, it got boring there," Maida said breezily. "More was happening here, so I packed up and flew home. Come in. It's freezing."

Poppy crossed the porch and entered the house just as Griffin was pulling on his parka. He called out a discreet "Did you have a good afternoon?"

Good was not a word Poppy would use to describe the afternoon's events, but suddenly she didn't even want to *think* about them. So she said to him, "Are you leaving?"

"I asked him to dinner," Maida put in, "but he said he had work to do." Poppy smelled something familiar cooking.

Griffin stretched the blue headband over his head. "You and your mom want time together."

Poppy was thinking that she wasn't sure about that, when a movement on the sofa caught her eye. She had forgotten about Victoria. She was sitting on Poppy's favorite chenille throw, arching her back, looking as though she'd just woken up.

"Did you meet my cat?" Poppy asked Maida.

"*Your* cat?" Griffin asked.

The words were barely out of his mouth when Victoria leaped off the sofa. With unerring aim she approached Poppy and jumped right up. Poppy's heart melted. Wool jacket and all, she wrapped her arms around the cat and buried her face in that soft orange fur. Unable to resist, she raised smug eyes to Griffin's.

"Okay," he said as he put on his boots. "That's it. A guy can only take so much rejection in one day. I'll leave you three ladies to yourselves." He went out, closing the door behind him.

Poppy stroked the cat's head with the finger of one hand and used the other to unwind her scarf. "So did you meet Victoria?"

"Oh yes. She woke up for that. Then she went back to sleep. She seems to be interested in you, only you." Maida smiled. "And so, my dear, does Griffin." She took the scarf out of Poppy's hand.

"Griffin," Poppy informed her, "is only interested in using my shower, my desk space, and my phone."

"He seems like a nice person," Maida mused. "I wish he weren't a reporter. But John's one, and Lily's doing fine with him. I suppose if I can live with one journalist son-in-law, I can live with a second."

"Don't get used to the idea, Mom. I am not marrying Griffin."

Maida held out a hand for Poppy's coat. "Oh, I know that, Poppy. You aren't getting married at all." She took the coat when Poppy slid out her arms, and she hung it on a hook by the door. "You've been saying that since you were five."

Poppy knew she was being humored, but it was odd coming from her mother. Maida was a perfectionist. She liked things just so. Typically she would have urged Poppy to encourage Griffin because, after all, getting married and having children was the ideal. That she didn't argue gave Poppy pause. Leaving a hand on Victoria, she went to the phone panel. "Oh my."

"What?"

"Griffin left a list of every call he answered. I need to use this man more." He had even switched on the audio so she would hear if another call came in. He had also left his own papers in a pile at the end of the desk, and his briefcase was on the floor nearby. It was either a statement of trust or an invitation for Poppy to take a look.

Not up for deciding which, she wheeled past the phone bank and followed the scent of bay leaves and sage down the hall to the kitchen. She opened the oven to peek. "Ahh." Poppy sighed with satisfaction. "No one does pot roast like you do."

"Nothing's fresh there," Maida cautioned, more her exacting self now. "I had to get everything from the freezer or the pantry, not that it's the season for Mary Joan's red potatoes anyway, so I had to use canned ones. But I walked in the door, put the meat in the microwave to defrost, and had it starting to cook before I unpacked."

Poppy was used to Maida's doting. She was forever sending Poppy cooked food, clothes, candy, and books. Still, Poppy was touched by the effort she made now. "You didn't have to do this."

"I wanted to." Maida grew serious. "It was lonely down there."

"But you have lots of friends."

"Friends aren't my girls."

Victoria jumped off Poppy's lap and went to her food.

"I take it she's an indoor cat," Maida said.

"I certainly wouldn't let her out."

"And Griffin brought her for you? What a sweet thing."

"Well, he didn't bring her for me, exactly. He brought her in to show her to me, and she seemed to like the place, so it made sense to let her stay. But it's just for the time being, until Griffin leaves."

Maida went on as though Poppy hadn't spoken. "He knew you needed a pet. He saw this one and knew you'd take care of it. He knew you would understand her special needs."

Poppy didn't like the sound of that. "What needs are those?"

"This cat's blind. That takes understanding. You know what it is to have special needs."

Poppy bristled. "The handicapped cat for the handicapped girl?"

"No," Maida replied with care. "The handicapped cat for the girl who understands. That's all I meant, Poppy."

But Poppy couldn't get the other out of her mind. "The handicapped cat for the handicapped girl," she repeated. She wondered if Griffin had thought that, too, and was suddenly furious that Maida had pointed it out. "Did you have to say that?"

"I didn't say it. You did. That wasn't what I had in mind."

"I've made a life here, Mom. I've gotten used to being in this chair, and part of the reason is that people around me don't even *notice* it. I don't know why you have to throw it in my face." She wheeled around and headed out of the kitchen.

"I didn't, Poppy," Maida called, following quickly.

"You did. You took something innocent on Griffin's part and made it into something so . . . so pathetic that it makes me feel like a cripple." Poppy wheeled her chair to face Maida. "No one else makes me feel that way. Why do you have to do it?"

Doing a one-eighty, she wheeled off into the weight room and pulled the door closed. For a minute she sat fuming. Then she heard a meow at the door. Poppy slid the door open for Victoria to slip through. The sight of the cat brought a whisper of calm.

Though Griffin watched the clock for much of the evening, he wasn't idle. After leaving Poppy's, he picked up sandwiches at Charlie's and shared them with Billy Farraway in the bob-house, then headed back to the cabin. With a three-quarter moon shining on a fresh coat of snow, the night was a deep, brilliant blue.

Inside the cabin, Griffin checked his watch. He made coffee and checked his watch. He opened the door, looked out, and checked his watch. When it was late enough, he got into the truck, drove to just the right spot, set his blinkers, and called Poppy.

"Hey," he said, feeling a lift at the sound of her voice. "Did I wake you?" She didn't sound so much sleepy as deep in thought.

"No. I'm awake." She sighed softly. "Lots on my mind. Uh, I thought you didn't have cell reception."

"I don't on the island. I'm sitting here in the truck on the side of the road at the exact spot where I know the reception starts."

"What time is it?" she asked, and must have looked at the clock because she answered herself. "Nearly eleven."

"I wanted to wait until your mother had gone back to her house. How did dinner go?"

There was a pause. "It was okay. Thank you for asking."

"She was perfectly lovely to me. But I sense that you and she don't always get along. I guess it's a usual mother-daughter thing."

"I guess," Poppy said, but her tone suggested something else was on her mind. "Griffin? I have to ask you something. Did you take this cat with me in mind?"

Griffin hesitated. "As in, I thought you'd want this cat?"

"As in," she pushed, "you thought it would be a good pairing. She's handicapped. I'm handicapped. Was that it?"

"No," he answered honestly. "I didn't take her from Charlotte with you in mind at all. I took her for myself because she . . . touched me. She deserves a good home."

"Because she's blind?"

"Yes. Maybe that."

"Is that how you feel about me?"

He chuckled. "Looks to me like you have a good home."

"But not a man. Not a relationship. So the same kind of sensitivity that makes you want to give a blind cat a home might be what's bringing you here to me. I just wanted you to know I'm not that hard up. I could be with someone if I wanted. There are lots of men who've been after me since the accident. I'm not desperate."

"I'm not either, Poppy. I could be dating lots of other women."

"Why aren't you?"

"Beats me!" he exclaimed. "They'd be a lot less prickly than you are. But prickly is fun. It's interesting. Those others don't intrigue me the way you do."

"It's curiosity, then? Wondering what it's like to do it with a paraplegic?"

"Oh, come off it, Poppy," he scolded. "You intrigue me because you think. You act. You do what you want. I've never aspired to make love to a paraplegic. I do aspire to make love to you."

She was silent for the longest time.

"Are you crying again?" he asked.

She sniffled. "It's been a rough day."

"Your visit with Heather?" When he heard something that sounded like a moan, he said, "I'm coming over."

"No." There were sniffles and then a half-wailed "I'm okay."

"Then tell me about Heather. Did she say something?"

"I don't know."

"What do you mean?"

"She might have. I just don't *know*," Poppy cried.

Quietly he asked, "Is she Lisa?"

Poppy didn't answer, and he didn't want to push. "Can I come over in the morning and make you breakfast?"

"I can make myself breakfast."

"I know that, but I like to cook, and the setup on Little Bear is primitive. So indulge me, Poppy. I make a terrific baked French toast. What do you say?"

"That sounds pretty good. I like French toast."

"Is eight too early?"

"No."

"It's a date, then." He instantly regretted his choice of words. When she didn't object, he was heartened. Gently he said, "When we're done, will you tell me what upset you so about Heather?"

There was a pause, then a quiet "We'll see." And an even quieter "Griffin? Thank you."

"For what?"

"Calling. Caring that I was upset. People don't usually do that."

"That, dollface," he quipped, because his heart was beating up a storm and he had to make light of the moment, "is because you put out messages saying that you're entirely self-sufficient. But it's nice to have someone do something for you once in a while, isn't it?"

"Yeah," she drawled, apparently agreeing that a lightening of emotions was needed. "Drive carefully."

"I will. Sleep well."

Poppy lay in the not quite dark of a night lit by the moon reflecting on snow. She wasn't thinking about Griffin, though she had for a while when she had first turned out the lamp. Nor was she thinking about Heather. She was thinking about Perry Walker.

He had been a handsome guy—six feet tall, sandy hair, laughing eyes, and a wide smile—the life of the party until the very moment of his death. He'd been telling her a joke, shouting over the growl of the snowmobile. The joke had likely been either off-color or politically incorrect, because Perry delighted in being irreverent. But the words had been lost in the horror of what had followed.

Poppy pictured Perry in the weeks before he'd died, then tried to picture what he would have been like if he had lived. She figured he would have had a whole slew of kids, not because of any major plan but out of sheer carelessness. He was a randy guy. She wondered what would have happened if the tables had been turned, if she had been the one to die. Would he have been the one to reform?

She felt a movement at her side. It was the cat, who walked to the edge of the bed and slipped to the floor. There she groomed herself, looking confident. Poppy wondered whether she had always been so deft or whether it came with blindness. The cat was certainly adventurous. Granted, having been unceremoniously passed from Charlotte to Griffin to Poppy, she hadn't had a choice about trying new things, but she had certainly done it with style.

Of course, Victoria wasn't weighed down by guilt.

Chapter Six

Wanting to work out and shower before Griffin arrived, Poppy was up early Monday. She went through her usual routine, first with weights for strength, then the bicycle for flexibility.

When she finished up, she settled in her chair and studied the parallel bars. Aside from being at waist height rather than overhead, they weren't terribly different from the monkey bars she had used on the playground when she was growing up. She could use the bars for stability while she swung one hip forward, then the next. She could teach her hips to do that. With practice it would work.

Poppy looked across the room. There on hooks were a pair of leg braces. They weren't pretty. And they were a major hassle to put on. She didn't know why she should use them when she could wheel herself around ever so smoothly.

Then she remembered Star Smith up in the woods.

• • •

"It's no mistake?" Griffin echoed. "Are you sure she said that?"

"Watch my lips." Poppy mouthed the three words. Her lips were licked clean of the syrup she had poured on his oven-baked French toast, which he had to admit was the best he'd ever made.

"That's pretty clear," he agreed. "She's Lisa, then?" When Poppy bent over and put her cheek to her knees, he felt a wrenching inside. "You're not going to cry again, are you?" he asked, fearful.

"No," she said quietly. "I just . . . feel . . . weary."

He stroked her head. Her dark hair was short, but it was soft and thick and clean. He ran his fingers through it.

"The question," she said, "is how the Heather I know could have killed Rob DiCenza—or *anyone*."

He spoke quietly. "That's the direction we take. We assume that Lisa is not the villain the DiCenzas make her out to be, and we try to find the reason she might have run him down. But there's a problem. My friend Ralph is hitting a wall. No one in California is willing to talk, and the only person we have on this end is Heather."

"She wouldn't tell Micah a thing."

"But she mouthed those words to you," Griffin said. "So there's an admission. I think we need another opinion. Can you get someone in to cover the phones while we go for a ride?"

Poppy and Griffin took separate cars. She insisted that it was easier this way, since the Blazer was equipped for her and her chair.

"Baloney," Griffin teased. "You don't want to be seen with me."

She hesitated, then admitted, "That, too." There was no reason everyone in town had to know they were working together.

Fortunately, Cassie's office was around a bend and out of sight from the center of town. It was in a small, pale blue house that had white trim and a large oak plaque hanging from the porch: CASSIE BYRNES, ATTORNEY-AT-LAW.

Cassie prided herself on being proactive and bold. She needed information on Lisa and knew that Griffin could help. Ideally, she would have approached him rather than the other way around. But she wouldn't have done it yet. She had a client coming in that morning, a woman who had agreed to seek a restraining order against an abusive boyfriend. She didn't have time to seek out Griffin. But Poppy had called, requesting a meeting, and Cassie trusted Poppy. So there was Griffin pulling into the driveway behind Poppy's Blazer.

Cassie watched him jog gallantly up to Poppy's door and give her a hand with the lift. It bothered her that her office was a god-awful mess. Cassie knew the Griffin type; she had gone to college and law school with them. Their image of law firms was of the rich male variety, with fine art, mahogany, marble, and Oriental rugs. Those firms hired assistants who were paid to type labels and organize files, but Cassie couldn't afford that. Her office was an eclectic collection of file cabinets, bookcases, and workspace, added to over the years as the need arose, and her walls were covered with the art of three children under the age of seven.

But Griffin merely smiled at the chaos and said an amused "Cool" before taking the seat Cassie had pointed him toward.

Then she forgot about the office, because Poppy told her what Heather had mouthed the afternoon before. Feeling a vast sadness, she let out a discouraged breath. "I suppose it makes sense. If it's true, we need to build a defense."

Griffin asked, "Legally, what happens if you admit in court that Heather is Lisa?"

"Immediately? She gets shipped back to California."

"Supposing that happens," he said. "What's her chance of bail?"

"For a capital case? None. Zero. Waste of breath unless we come up with something so strong that it makes everyone think twice."

"Like what?" Poppy asked.

"Like Heather having reason to fear for her life. Like she was threatened or battered. The problem is we'd need a witness."

"Big problem," Griffin injected. "From what I hear, everyone who might have known Lisa has been reached by the DiCenzas. No one's talking. So if there was a witness to anything, he or she is not coming forward. And then there's the PR war. Lisa's lost it unless we change something fast."

Cassie sat back and folded her arms. "What do you suggest?"

"A private meeting between Heather and me," Griffin said.

"Private? Poppy and I are her friends. Micah's her lover. Why would she tell you things she wouldn't tell any of us?"

"Why can a wife tell a therapist things she can't tell her husband? Because there's a neutrality to it. There isn't the fear of censure. Heather cares what you think of her. Me, I'm nothing to her."

Cassie had to admit there was an element of truth in what he said. But he wasn't saying it all. "You're a writer," she said. "What's in it for you?"

Poppy smirked. "Me. He wants to impress me. He's not writing about this." The smirk gave way to entreaty. "Cassie, he has resources that we don't."

"Like what?" Cassie asked.

"Like private investigators who owe me favors," he said. "Rob abused women. Lisa sought medical treatment at least twice."

Cassie arched a brow. "You can tie his battering to her

seeking treatment? Do you have someone who'll testify to the connection? Because that's what we need. If you can't get firsthand evidence, Heather would be just as well off claiming she isn't Lisa at all."

"Which brings us full circle," Poppy said. "Griffin wants to talk with her. Will you set up a meeting?"

Cassie wasn't sure Griffin would get anything more from Heather than the rest of them had. The psychiatrists she had talked with said that if Heather was suffering from post-traumatic stress disorder, the truth might be buried too deep to be unearthed without significant therapy. Cassie couldn't afford to hire a psychiatrist, nor could she afford to hire a private investigator. If Griffin would help out for free, far be it from Cassie to object.

"When do you want to go?" she asked Griffin as she reached for the phone.

As Micah turned off the lake road and came down his drive, he saw the dark sedan at his house. Two FBI agents were on the front porch; one of them carried Heather's computer. Pulling up sharply, Micah stepped from the truck. "That was fast," he said.

"We figured you needed it."

"Wrong. You searched the thing and found nothing. The only stuff in there has to do with my work."

"And Lisa's."

"There's no Lisa here. That's Heather's work."

"You're playin' with words. Where do you want this?"

Micah didn't budge. "I want it where it was when you took it."

The agents exchanged looks, then came down the porch steps, heading around to the back. Micah followed only until he could see the sugarhouse. Stopping there, he waited, and as he did that, two things ran through his mind: *There's no Lisa here*, Micah had said. *That's Heather's work*. The agent replied, *You're playin' with words*.

I'm Heather Malone, Heather had insisted during that first meeting at the courthouse. It struck him that she'd been playing with words, too, which led to the second thing that hit him. He felt a sudden, intense desire to see what was in that backpack.

When the agents emerged, he watched them walk past and drive off, and he would have gone straight to the woodpile the instant the car was out of sight if another car hadn't passed it on the way in.

Pulling up on the near side of his truck, his bookkeeper, Camille Savidge, rolled down her window. She shot a quick glance behind and asked, "Is everything all right?"

He grunted. "They returned the computer. My guess? The insides are gone. Wiped clean."

Camille held up a handful of disks. "I can fix that. And I can do whatever accounting you need."

Anyone else, and he would have just turned and walked off. But a man didn't do that with Camille. She was too decent a person. So he said, "I'm okay," and prayed that she would leave.

"Can you restore these yourself?"

"Nah. I'll work the way I used to."

"But if you don't know what's on the disks—"

"I'll manage."

"How?"

As civilly as he could, given the impatience he felt, he said, "I'll *manage*. Can we talk about this another time? I have to work."

"Let me help, Micah. I don't have anything to do until later. I want to help."

"Can you get Heather out of jail?" he threw back. "Can you prove she isn't Lisa? Can you explain to Missy and Star why someone who says she loves them can hide secrets so bad she can't speak up to save her life? Can you explain it to *me?* I can't deal with this, Camille. Heather and I had a good life. I want it back."

The stricken look on her face made him regret the outburst. Not that he'd had any control. He had kept too much locked up inside. Unable to analyze that or to think about Heather for another second, Micah strode off. He had tubing to lay in the sugar bush.

Poppy drove around for a bit. It was too early for lunch, and she realized she was in the mood to be by herself. So she drove all the way around the lake with no radio, only the shush of the tires where melting snow wet the road.

When she was back in the center of town, she pulled in at the church. The spire was sunlit and gloriously white against a clear blue sky. She studied it awhile, then put the car in gear again and drove onto the narrow road that wound through the town cemetery. When she crested a small rise, her breathing grew shallow.

Pulling over onto the snowy berm, she let the Blazer idle. Inexorably, her eye was drawn past a dozen granite markers of different sizes and shapes to a simple but handsome one that stood in the back, looking very much apart and alone.

Perry Walker had died young, and though there was space here for others of his family, they were all still alive. Perry's parents lived in Elkland now, forty minutes to the north. She didn't know whether any of Perry's siblings were still in New Hampshire. She didn't want to know.

Even now she felt a great yawing inside, the need to escape. But her eyes clung to that stone, to the carved letters that were visible even from where she sat, as though someone had wanted her to be able to see them from the road, to read, remember, and regret. Yes, she wanted to run away. More, though, she wanted to talk to Perry.

But the thought of saying certain things aloud, even to a dead man, terrified her. So she shifted gears and gave the Blazer some gas. When Perry called out to her, she accelerated. In no time she had left his gravestone behind. She exited the cemetery, but that didn't mean she was done. She and Perry had unfinished business.

Griffin had no problems getting into the jail. Cassie had phoned ahead so that not only was he expected, he was given the privacy of a lawyer-client meeting room. When the door opened and Heather was let in, he extended a hand. "I'm Griffin Hughes, Poppy's friend. Poppy and Cassie agreed that I should come. Want to sit?"

She ignored the invitation and stood by the door. "Why aren't they here?" she asked unsteadily.

"They thought you'd feel more comfortable with just me."

She didn't look comfortable at all. She looked frightened.

Griffin took a seat. "Here's the thing," he said gently. "We don't have any leads about where you were before you came to Lake Henry. You can say that you're Heather Malone all you want, but unless we get proof, it isn't worth anything. Lisa Matlock left California fifteen years ago. We need proof that you were Heather Malone before then. Paperwork will do it. Same with a witness—a friend, relative, co-worker. Lawyers use the word 'corroboration.' "

"You're not a lawyer," she said in the same shaky voice.

"No. I'm a writer. But I'm not here to write. I'm here as a friend because I think I can help. I have a network of contacts; they'll do favors for me. It won't cost you a cent."

She didn't look any more at ease.

"So what we need," he went on in the same gentle voice, "is corroborative evidence. Ideally we'd look for evidence on Heather Malone, but you won't talk. You won't give us a lead. So this is what we're going to do. We're going to look at it from the other end—from the Lisa end. We're going to try to figure out why Lisa Matlock ran down Rob DiCenza."

"If you're going after Lisa, what do you want from me?"

"A name. A date. A place. See, the DiCenza family has gotten to most of the people who knew anything about Rob and Lisa, so no one's talking. What I know is this: I know that Rob was abusive. Lisa made several trips to area ERs under assumed names, and she always denied the abuse. I don't think she meant to kill Rob. She may not have seen him. It was a field. There were cars parked all over that night, and he probably just darted out from between them. I don't think she planned to hit him. I don't even think she knew he was dead. But she knew how powerful his family was, so once she learned he was dead, she just kept going and fled.

"And I don't blame her," he continued. "The DiCenzas had power, and she had none. She knew—rightly—that her story wouldn't be believed. But someone had to have seen something in that relationship. Rob was a party boy. Someone had to have seen or heard something to suggest that he was less than a gentleman."

"If the witnesses wouldn't talk then, why will they talk now?"

"Fifteen years have passed. That's a long time for guilt to be eating at someone who may have lied. Or that person may have a gripe against the DiCenzas now, one that he didn't have then."

She thought about that, then said quietly, "What's the use?"

"Are you kidding?" he asked. "The alternative is spending the rest of your life in prison."

Her eyes welled up.

He pressed on. "Maybe that doesn't bother you, but it will bother your friends. They're in your corner all the way. They love you. The longer you stay silent, the more you let them down."

Her chin trembled, but he refused to soften the words.

Finally she cried, "What do you *want* from me?"

"Just what I said before: A name. A date. A place. I want something that relates either to Heather or to Lisa, something suggesting that the people in California are wrong."

She covered her face with her hands.

"Hate me, Heather," he challenged, needing to push her that little bit more, "but what you're doing is selfish. You aren't the only one involved here. If you can't do something for your friends, do it for Micah and Missy and Star. Your silence is hurting *them*."

For a minute she just stood there with her hands over her face. It took all of Griffin's self-control not to say something that would give her an out. He waited first one minute, then another.

Finally she dropped her hands. "Aidan Greene," she said in a monotone, and spelled it out. "A-I-D-A-N G-R-E-E-N-E."

Griffin didn't have to write down the name; it was instantly burned into his mind. "Where can I find him?"

"Now? I don't know."

"Fifteen years ago?"

"Sacramento." Her eyes grew woeful with the admission.

He smiled sadly, rose, and went to her. Gently he squeezed her shoulder and said, "Thank you, Heather. This will help."

• • •

Micah returned from the sugar bush earlier than he might have. As the afternoon wore on and he stretched coil after coil of tubing from one tree to the next, the issue of the knapsack loomed large.

Inside the sugarhouse, he went to the pile of wood and uncovered the worn canvas pack. This time his need to know what was inside was greater than his fear of what he would find. Undoing the buckles, he opened the sack. There were three envelopes inside.

One contained three photographs. They were black-and-white shots, the same two young women in each. They couldn't have been more than teenagers. There was something familiar about their faces. Micah imagined he saw traces of Heather. Mother and aunt? Grandmother and great-aunt? There was no writing anywhere, no date, no notation of any sort.

Replacing the photographs, he turned to the other envelopes. The thinner of the two bore the return address of a law firm in Chicago. He took out the letter it held and read it once, then again. Then he opened the last envelope. Inside were two plastic ID bracelets of the kind that hospitals used. The larger had Heather's name on it, the smaller that of Baby Girl Malone.

That was it, then. Heather had had a baby six months before coming to Lake Henry and had given it up for adoption through a Chicago law firm.

Micah let out a long, pent-up breath. He should have been angry. Heather hadn't been willing to have *his* baby, though she knew he wanted it. Now he could only figure that she had left part of her heart with this child, who for whatever reason she had to give up.

He was trying to think what that reason might be, when he heard the crunch of boots on packed-down snow. He looked up as Griffin came through the door.

It didn't occur to him to hide the knapsack. Griffin might be an outsider, but there was something about him that put Micah at ease.

Griffin spoke first. "Do you know a man named Aidan Greene?"

"No." Micah passed Griffin the envelopes. "These were inside her knapsack. She's had it hidden since she moved in with me."

Griffin looked at the photographs first, just as Micah had. Then he read the law-firm letter and examined the ID bracelets. When his eyes rose to Micah's, they were eager. "Looks like both of us hit pay dirt today." He told Micah about his talk with Heather. "A law firm can be called. Hospital records can be examined. This is a start."

Micah tried to share his eagerness, but the fear was back. A door had opened on Heather's past. He was terrified to learn where it would lead.

Early Tuesday morning Griffin awoke to the sun slanting in through the cabin window. He hadn't pulled the café curtains the night before. He rarely did. Privacy was a city need. Here no one looked in. On Little Bear he had his own corner of the world.

After he ate breakfast, Griffin set off for town. He stopped by the general store long enough to fill his mug with coffee and catch the pulse of the town before heading for Micah's. He arrived just as Micah was returning home from dropping the girls at school.

Griffin climbed from the cab of his truck. "I gave the information to my investigator," he said as he fell into step beside the taller man. "He'll call when he learns something. Need any help here?"

Micah shot him a look that reflected the general sentiment at Charlie's. Sugaring season was coming on fast. With the sun strong for a second day in a row, snow was melting, icicles were dripping, and the air was gentler on the lungs—all of which created a sense of urgency for Micah, who now needed to finish laying tubing through the sugar bush in a handful of days. The race was on; everyone knew Micah was putting people off right and left. He didn't want them there, he claimed. He could manage himself. He didn't need favors.

Truth be told, Griffin was doing himself a favor by coming. He had suffered through another tedious talk with Prentiss Hayden the evening before and on principle wasn't working on the politician's bio today. He wanted to be outside in the fresh air.

The two men went to the sugarhouse, where they loaded the truck with coils of piping. Then they headed up the hill, climbing steadily to a point high above the lake.

As soon as they left the truck, Micah was all business. He shouldered several coils of the blue plastic tubing and strapped on a waist pack with tools. "See that black tubing?" he asked.

Griffin did. It skirted the area in which they were headed.

"That's the mainline," Micah explained. "It stays up year-round. Leaving it here takes some care, but it's easier than taking it down."

Griffin could understand why. The mainline was held in place by a system of steel posts, cable wires, and small plastic ties, the latter affixed every foot. Every foot. In a fifty-acre spread? He couldn't begin to count the number of ties used in all.

"End of season," Micah went on, "after I've flushed the thing out, I cover the openings with tape. What we're putting in now is the lateral line. It carries sap from trees to mainline. Mainline takes it down the hill to the sugarhouse."

After tying one end of the thin blue tubing around the tree farthest from the mainline, Micah stretched it to the next closest tree, then the next, maximizing the tension to hold the tubing in place. From time to time he indicated that Griffin should brace a section until the tension picked up.

Tying no more than four trees to each mainline connection, the two men finished one area, moved to the next, finished that one, and drove on. The truck was nearly empty when a cell phone rang.

Griffin reached into his pocket, but Micah's hand was the one that came up with the ringer. "Yeah," he said into it. "Nothing. . . . No. . . . Twenty minutes." He dropped the phone back into his pocket and set off with the last coil. "Poppy has lunch at the house."

Griffin felt anticipation not only for the twenty minutes it took to finish laying the last coil and drive back down to the house, but through lunch. All he had to do was to look at Poppy and he felt a lift. Her eyes were a warm brown, her cheeks pink, her hair adorably messy. She smiled easily and insisted that Griffin eat the half of her tuna sandwich that she claimed she couldn't finish.

After lunch Poppy wheeled over to Micah, who stood by the table brooding, his brow furrowed and his eyes on the floor.

"We didn't talk about the baby thing," she said quietly. "Are you okay with that?"

He raised somber eyes. "No. She should've told me."

Poppy agreed. But she could see Heather's side, too. "Her past involved another man. Maybe she felt you didn't want to hear that."

"I knew she'd been with a man before me. I'm not stupid. And she wasn't in love with another man when she came here. I knew that. So why couldn't she tell me about the baby?"

"Maybe she associated the baby with the man. It was part

of her past," Poppy repeated. "It was over and done. Why did she have to tell you that?"

"Because she loved me," Micah answered. "You don't keep secrets like that from someone you love. Having a baby is a big thing for a woman. How could she never say a word about it?"

"Maybe she just couldn't."

"I can't buy couldn't."

But Poppy knew it was possible. "You said it yourself. Having a baby is a big thing for a woman. Having to give it up could be even bigger. There are all sorts of emotions tied up with that."

"She could have said it was a hard pregnancy and she couldn't survive another one. She could have said that after giving one baby up, she couldn't bear to have another. I wouldn't have agreed with her, but it would have been better than her saying nothing."

Poppy sat back. She didn't know where to go with the discussion, particularly with Griffin sitting right there. "Maybe we need to break the ice," she said. "Let her know it's okay."

"I don't know if I can say it's okay," Micah confessed.

The statement disturbed Poppy. "You can't forgive her?"

He didn't answer.

Micah was a good person. He was honest and decent and loyal. If he wasn't capable of forgiveness, Poppy didn't want to know. "Can we talk about this another time?" she asked.

He frowned and gave a short nod.

Poppy didn't say a word. She couldn't. Her throat was too tight.

On Wednesday night Poppy invited Griffin for dinner, though when the time came around, she was having second thoughts. She had showered, put on a silk shirt and black jeans, and fiddled with her hair and her eyes and her cheeks—all things that she absolutely should not have done lest he think this was a date.

But she owed him for helping Micah, and he was coming here each day to shower anyway, with or without news to report about Heather, and he had a right to see his cat, though Poppy had absolutely no intention of letting him take the cat to Princeton. Besides, Poppy liked him.

So she set two places in the kitchen and had just finished checking on the Rock Cornish hen in the oven when he showed up fresh from the shower. He looked delightfully damp, smelled decidedly good, produced a bottle of wine, and promptly uncorked it.

"We're celebrating," he announced, filling two glasses. "Ralph found Aidan Greene."

Poppy's eyes opened wide. There were so many things to ask, along with the fear of asking any of them. So she settled for a simple "Oh my."

Griffin smiled as he handed her a glass. "Micah had the exact same ambivalence on his face when he heard."

Poppy didn't want to hear anything bad, but there might be something good. So she asked a cautious "Is he someone we want to acknowledge?"

"My guess is yes. Aidan Greene was Rob DiCenza's best friend."

Poppy's heart sank. "Well then, he *won't* help."

"He wouldn't at the time of the accident." Griffin opened the oven and peered inside. "This smells incredible." He closed the door and straightened. "At the time, Aidan Greene said he was in the men's room that night and nowhere near the field of cars when the accident happened. Less than a year after that, though, he pretty much disappeared. He had a great job with the DiCenza Foundation in Sacramento, but he quit it, moved away, let friendships die. That's why we had a hard time finding him."

"So where is he?"

"Minneapolis. He's a school counselor. He has a wife and kids and lives a quiet, careful life there."

Poppy took a drink of her wine. "Why do we think he'll say anything different now from what he said then?"

Griffin opened the oven again, reached for mitts, and pulled out the pan. "This is done," he said, and started filling each plate with half a hen, roasted potatoes, and an array of vegetables. "Because people don't just suddenly settle into obscurity unless there's a reason for it. Maybe he couldn't live with the DiCenza restraints. Maybe he didn't like being told to keep quiet."

"If that's so, wouldn't he have already gone to the police? He must read the papers. He must know that Heather's been arrested."

Griffin put a plate at each of the table settings. "He may need a push. Ralph'll approach the guy tomorrow. If he strikes out, I'll go." He gestured her to the table. "I'm sorry to be so impatient, but I am starved. May I help you with your chair, madam?"

Poppy couldn't help but smile.

She was still smiling later that evening. The food was gone. The wine was gone. The table was gone, or more aptly, they were gone from it and had settled into the sofa by the fire. Even Poppy's chair was gone, off to the side where she couldn't see it, so that she could pretend she was as physically able as the next. Harry Connick, Jr., crooned softly. The fire blazed and popped.

Griffin turned his head against the sofa back and caught up

her hand. He didn't do anything with it, just laced his fingers through hers. It felt nice enough, safe enough. So Poppy didn't pull away.

"Want a kiss?" He dug into his pocket with a free hand.

"No. No kiss. I'm stuffed."

He settled in again. "Tell me about the accident."

Her eyes flew to his. She returned a dry "Tell me what you already know."

He smiled. "There was a party with a big bonfire up in the hills. You'd all gone by snowmobile, and there was lots of booze. You and Perry left. The snowmobile took a turn too fast and hit a boulder. You were both thrown off. Perry was killed. You lived."

Staring into the fire, Poppy allowed herself to recall it. "I didn't want to at first. Didn't want to live. If we'd only been a few feet to one side or the other, we'd both be whole."

"You're whole." He took her hand to his chest. "Were you and Perry in love?"

"I don't think so. We were lovers. But it wouldn't have lasted. We were too alike. We had the same wild streak, the same need to rebel. Neither one of us could temper the other."

"Do you think about him often?"

"I try not to. But I've thought about him more since you've come."

"I want to think that's because I'm the first man you've let come close since him."

She didn't say anything.

"So where's it going, Poppy? I'd like to kiss you, but I don't dare, because you could as easily chew me out as kiss me back."

She wouldn't chew him out, she decided.

"You told Micah," he said, "that he might have to break the ice and say the things that Heather couldn't. If I were to do that with you, I'd say that you do like me, but you don't feel you have a right to do some of the things that you want. It's a kind of punishment. For Perry."

Poppy took her hand back, still laced with his, and studied their fingers. "He's dead, and I'm alive. I may be punishing myself."

"How long does the punishment go on? It was an accident."

"It could have been prevented. If we'd been going slower, if we'd had less to drink. We thought we were immortal."

"We all feel immortal at that age. And it's not like you punish yourself in everything, Poppy. You've made a good life. You just won't allow yourself to go beyond a certain point."

Her eyes met his. "What point?"

"Skiing. Snowmobiling. Having a husband and kids."

"Griffin, I do have limitations. I'll never be able to walk. Or dance. Even if I got past all that guilt, there'd be the guilt of knowing that if I get involved with a guy, I'd be holding him back."

"That's a crock, Poppy." In a second Griffin was going to the stereo, switching CDs. By the time he was back, the opening bars of Collin Raye's "In This Life" were filling the room.

He hunkered down in front of her. "I want to show you how we can dance, but you have to trust me."

Poppy did trust him. But she was frightened.

Before she could say no, he slipped his hands under her and lifted her. "Put your arms around my neck," he said, but they were already there, gone up naturally, only in part to fight the fear. Holding her against him, he began to sway to the music.

"Relax," he whispered after the first turn, and how could Poppy not? She loved the music, loved the confident way Griffin held her—and she loved to dance. She let her body feel the beat, let it slide through her shoulders and her chest. Dropping her cheek to his shoulder, she moved with him. Their bodies were totally in sync.

Poppy was just getting started when the song ended. "Replay it," she ordered giddily. This time she was into the song from start to finish, meeting his eyes, smiling in delight. He kissed that smile and took her breath away. She was feeling dizzy when he drew back.

"Don't stop," she whispered, and sliding her hands into his hair, she returned his kiss. She didn't protest when he lowered her to the sofa and kissed her there or when he touched her breasts.

She felt incredibly alive. After being twelve years without, she was stunned. The sensation was stronger than she had imagined. Perhaps her breasts had become more sensitive to make up for a numbness below. The thing was, below didn't feel numb. Oh, it wasn't the same as she remembered, but it felt incredibly full.

Then Griffin drew back again. His cheeks were flushed; his eyes were the deepest blue she'd ever seen. She started to laugh.

Those eyes went wide. "This is not a laughing matter."

She cupped his cheek and ran her thumb over the barest shadow of the bruise he had gotten his first day in town. "I'm sorry. It's just that you warned me back in October. You said your eyes were dark blue during sex. I mean, this isn't sex, not really, but they are."

"Why isn't this sex?" he asked.

"Because it isn't—you know—the whole thing and all."

He drew in an uneven breath. "That is through no lack of desire on my part." Hitching himself up on his elbows, he said in the gentlest, most sensual voice, "If you don't want to do this now, I won't push you beyond what you want to give. This is too important."

Absurdly, she felt tears in her eyes.

"There's a price, though," he said. "I know about Thursdays at Charlie's Back Room. I want to go. Be my date?"

Chapter Seven

Charlie's Back Room had been a Lake Henry tradition for more years than anyone but the oldest of the old-timers could count. The small raised stage hadn't changed, nor had the café tables and chairs, nor had the potbelly stove that exuded a welcome warmth in the cold. The place still smelled of old barn board, now mixed with the aroma of coffee. Best of all, in Poppy's opinion, was the wafting scent of chocolate-chip cookies baked from Charlie's grandmother's recipe and served warm from the oven.

Tonight's headliner was a string quartet of fiftysomething players who did the Beatles on violin, viola, cello, and bass. Poppy loved the Beatles. Apparently Griffin did, too. So she used that excuse in explaining his presence with her that night.

"He's a die-hard Beatles fan," she told everyone. "He's been helping Micah all week. I figured we owe him this."

Griffin remained at Poppy's side, quiet and amiable, letting her make the introductions, ask the questions, take the lead in conversation. After a bit she began directing the conversation his way.

It was an easy transition because the talk turned to sugaring. Since Micah wasn't there, Griffin gave a status report on the tubing. He said that Micah could use help in the sugar bush—and Poppy hoped that the invitation would bring offers. But there were only sympathetic nods. Micah had offended too many of the townsfolk.

Griffin seemed comfortable, Poppy realized. He could find something to talk about with anyone who approached. With Cassie's husband, Mark, it was Princeton, from which it turned out they had both graduated. With John Kipling it was mutual friends in Boston.

On Poppy's side there was inevitable speculation. Cassie began by scolding her in a whisper, "You didn't *tell* me you were coming with him."

"I didn't know," Poppy whispered back. "It was a last-minute thing. He loves the Beatles."

"Yeah, yeah, yeah," Cassie teased.

Poppy's sister Lily was just as curious. When Griffin and John began to talk, she pulled a chair close to Poppy. "You're wearing mascara. What does that mean?"

Poppy laughed. "I needed a pick-me-up. It's been a bad week, worrying about Heather. But if you're thinking I did it for Griffin, think again. He's a friend, Lily. That's all."

"I'm sorry it isn't more. It should be, with a guy like that. He's perfect for you."

"No. He's Ivy League. He's media. He's *rich*, for heaven's sake."

"Oh, Poppy," Lily scolded under her breath, "so are we."

"Why does everyone think I *need* someone?" Poppy asked. "Am I not functioning well enough alone?"

"You're functioning very well," Lily said. "I've been watching the two of you since you got here. You may think he's absorbed, talking with John or Charlie, but he keeps looking back at you, like you're his center, his *anchor.* He wants to be near you, Poppy."

"Well, of course he does. I'm his entrée here, his protection."

Lily shook her head with conviction. "That's not what I see."

"Well, it's what *I* see," Poppy insisted, and glanced around on the verge of a snit. "Is there a reason why everyone is harping on this? Tell me something that doesn't have to do with Griffin."

"I'm pregnant."

Poppy caught in a breath.

Incredibly, so did Lily. Her eyes were suddenly open wide, like she couldn't believe what she'd just said.

"Close your mouth," Poppy chided in a whisper and, grinning, gave her a hug. "What incredible news!"

"No one else knows," Lily said against her ear. "I mean, other than John. I'm just six weeks along. I wasn't going to tell you yet."

Poppy held her back. "I am *so* happy for you."

Lily's eyes held worry. "Are you? I've had so many good things come my way in the last few months. I feel guilty sometimes."

"Oh, Lily, you deserve it all," Poppy said, meaning every word. "You've suffered through ugly times. It's your turn."

"And you?" Lily asked ever so gently. "When's yours?"

Griffin was in a corner of the general store, which was closed now, and quiet in contrast to the Back Room. He had to come here to call in his flight arrangements to Minneapolis. Aidan Greene was refusing to talk. Griffin wanted to have a go at him himself. He looked around as a woman emerged from the shadows; then he smiled and put out his hand. "I'm Griffin. And you're Camille."

Camille Savidge was an attractive woman in her fifties, with chocolate-colored eyes, fair skin that remained dewy and smooth, and a head of gray hair. She dressed simply and in muted colors, but there was an elegance to her that set her apart. In her own quiet way, as bookkeeper, accountant, and computer person, she was involved in the lives of half of Lake Henry.

That was what Charlie had told Griffin several mornings before, when Camille had whisked past them, emerging from the office and out the front door. Tonight was the first time Griffin and she had formally met.

"Do you have a minute?" Camille asked him.

Distant chatter came from the Back Room. "Of course."

"It's about Heather. I know that Cassie is donating her time, and they say that you're not charging, either, but Micah is strapped. I have a kitty. If you need something, please let me know."

Griffin was touched. "That's very generous."

"I've always liked Heather." She grew hesitant. "Does she have a chance of beating this?"

"I'll know more in a few days. I'm heading out tomorrow morning. There may be someone with new information."

Camille seemed to want to ask more, but she simply pressed her lips together and nodded.

Griffin, of course, was curious about Camille's involvement. "Are you close to Heather?"

Camille smiled. "We're good friends. I worked with her when she first came to town. I was happy when she and Micah got together."

"Do you know about her past?"

"She doesn't talk about that. But if I can help you find

something to help Heather, I want to do it. Will you let me know?"

Griffin nodded.

"Thank you," she said, and went off as quietly as she had come.

Poppy kept a nonchalant eye on the door and was relieved when Griffin finally appeared. She didn't want him missing a single song. She wanted him beside her through it all.

He slipped into his chair as the string ensemble finished warming up. Then the fun began. Songs like "Yesterday," "Norwegian Wood," and "Strawberry Fields Forever" seemed made for strings, and this group played them well. The show ended with a prolonged version of "Let It Be." By the time the last note sounded, the crowd was on its feet, and the applause was deafening.

Afterward Poppy and Griffin said their good-byes and went out to the Blazer. They didn't say much as Poppy drove home, and when they got there, he asked simply, "Can I come in?"

She was terrified. But she couldn't have kept him out if her life had depended on it.

He must have sensed that, because by the time he came to her side to help her out, he said, "Let's go down to the lake first."

"It'll be cold," she warned, but she figured that the cold was the point. There had been heat in that car, far beyond what the Blazer produced. He was slowing things down. She was grateful for that.

Reaching in, he tied her scarf around the collar of her jacket, then picked her up and carried her through the snow down to the lake.

Poppy hadn't been out on the lakeshore at night since the first snow of the season. "Any other season," she said, "and I do this by myself. There's a dock and a system of ramps. I wheel myself down into the water, slip out of my chair, and swim off."

"I bet you're a good swimmer."

"I'm a good swimmer."

They reached the edge of the lake. "I'm surprised you don't go south for the winter so that you can swim year-round," he said.

"Like the loons?" she asked.

"Like the loons. When'll they be back?"

"In April. Within hours of ice-out. For days you watch the ice getting thinner and thinner until it's black. Then it gets porous and just breaks up and goes away. The loons land within hours of that."

The moon was behind gnarled fingers of clouds, but that didn't take anything from the charm of the night. Yes, it was cold, but she was sheltered against Griffin. Besides, the cold was half the fun.

"Another week," she mused, "and the moon will be full. This time of year it's the Maple Moon. Sugar Moon is what Native Americans called it. Did I tell you about sugar-on-snow?"

He grinned. "I don't believe you did."

"If you take hot new syrup and drizzle it on snow, it hardens into chewy strings. We make a party of it during sugaring. Chewy syrup, raised doughnuts, and a sour pickle. One taste works off the other to enhance all three." Smiling, she tucked her nose in the warm spot just below his ear. He smelled of her aloe soap. It was light and fresh, not feminine at all.

Griffin then began the short trek to the house. Poppy moved her lips up and pressed a kiss where her nose had been. He didn't say a word, but she heard the catch of his breath.

At the house, he went in the door, kicked it shut behind

him, and carried her down the hall to her bedroom. In laying her on the bed, their bodies came apart, and she saw the hunger in his eyes.

She hadn't seen a hunger like that in more than a dozen years. He untied her scarf and unzipped her jacket. Tossing his own jacket aside, he crossed his arms, reached for the hem of his sweater, and whipped it off along with the shirt underneath.

Poppy wasn't prepared for that. She quite helplessly put a hand out. Fingers spread, she slid her palm over lean muscle and ribs.

He took her mouth then with the same hunger she had seen in his eyes, and how could she not answer it? She felt a tingling and could have sworn it was in her lower body.

His mouth stroked hers again and again, deepening the kiss slowly, steadily. It was unbelievably arousing. Poppy arched her back, and suddenly he had her sweater up and over her head.

He looked. He touched. The ripples of heat that he caused traveled deep, so deep that she would have writhed had she had the mobility. She loved the thickness of his wavy hair, loved the strength of his neck, loved the way his muscles bunched—back, shoulders, chest—when she touched them. Needing to feel his belly, she pushed her fingers down under the waistband of his jeans.

When he made a choked sound, she stopped short.

"Don't," he said hoarsely.

Horrified, she pulled her hands up and away.

"Don't *stop*," he pleaded, but the words seemed forced to her.

She tucked her hands under the pillows.

He drew her over to face him. "What happened?" he asked.

"You made a sound, like more was happening than you wanted."

"That sound was because not *enough* was happening." He caught her mouth and kissed her. "Are you afraid?" he asked.

She was terrified, but how could she say that?

His smile was exquisitely gentle. "I think you are. I think you're afraid you won't feel what you want to feel. You're afraid it won't work. You're afraid I'll be turned off. Is that it?"

He did understand, after all. Her chin wobbled, but she nodded.

"Trust me. I won't have that problem," he said in a voice that had grown raspy. His eyes were on her face. "You are just so beautiful."

"But not—" she cried.

"Not where? Your legs?" He ran a hand down. "You can't feel that, Poppy, but I do, and they feel just right." The backs of his fingers brushed their way up her body until the sensation was so strong that she closed her eyes, put her head back, drew in a breath.

"Your body's working," he whispered, "so I'm thinking that the problem is emotional. I'm thinking that you feel guilty doing this."

She did, indeed, but she wanted this now. Taking his face in her hands, she kissed him. Immersing herself in the pleasure it brought, she pushed guilt away, pushed fear away, until all that remained was the feeling. She kept it up while he removed the rest of her clothes, and it was so intense that she was suddenly the impatient one, pushing away his clothes just to get him closer.

If he was unusually slow or gentle or careful, she didn't know it, because she loved what he did. It was a miracle.

It was the best thing that had happened to her since wheelchairs with mag wheels—which was what she told Griffin when his wristwatch beeped at five the next morning.

He was not pleased.

• • •

Griffin didn't like the hour, didn't like the darkness. He didn't like the fact that he was booked on a six-thirty flight to Minneapolis. What really bothered him, though, was the word "thing." "The best *thing* since mag wheels? I don't call what we did a *thing*."

"What would you call it?"

"The best experience of my life," he said. They were lying face to face. He reached out to touch her, thought twice about it, pulled back. "Can't do this now. Gotta get up. I have a plane to catch."

Defying him, she wrapped her hand around his neck and brought him close for a kiss, and it fired him up all over again. How could he stop? She wanted him. If she wanted to call it sex, fine. If she wanted to call it a thing, that was fine, too. Yes, he had to catch a plane, but satisfying her was more important.

Afterward he scooped her up and took her into the shower. The grab bars that lined the shower stall offered a perfect little ledge for propping her up while he soaped her, while she soaped him, while they kissed and touched. Then he wrapped her in a towel, set her out of the stall, and let her watch while he hurriedly dressed.

"I am so late," he said as he tugged on his jeans, "but it's been worth every second. I guessed it would be that way the first time I laid eyes on you—no, even before that. I felt it on the phone."

"You did not," she chided, but she was smiling widely.

"I did. There was something between us right from the start. You are unique, Poppy."

She patted the arm of her chair. "I am that."

Pushing his arms into the sleeves of his shirt, he fastened two buttons while he chose his words. Then he put his hands on the arms of her chair and put his face level with hers.

"This chair is part of who you are. I have no problem with that. I don't see that it interferes with anything I want in a woman. I love you, Poppy."

Her smile faded. Her eyes grew sad. She shook her head slowly and pleaded in a whisper, "Don't say that. Don't spoil this."

"I was hoping to make it even better," he teased, desperate even for a smile. "I haven't ever said those words to a woman before."

She didn't reply.

He finished buttoning his shirt. "Don't feel you have to say anything," he remarked. "Telling a person you love him is big stuff. I wouldn't want you saying it unless you felt it, which clearly you don't now. I just wanted you to know how I felt. I gotta go."

Micah was putting in spiles. He remembered the old days, when metal spouts were hammered into the trees and buckets were hung directly below. His spiles were plastic now. Each had two feet of thin plastic tubing already attached and hanging down, thanks to the work he'd done late nights for the last few weeks.

Sleep? He didn't need sleep. The sun was high; the snow was thinning. Another few days and the sap would flow. And here he was, just putting in the first of the spiles. Using a drill, he made a hole that angled slightly up as it went in, so that the sap would drip down. Once the hole was made, he inserted the spile and tapped it in. He knew how hard to tap and did it with an economy of motion. Once the connection was made, he moved on to the next tree.

A gruff voice startled him with a loud "Hey."

He looked around fast. Billy Farraway stood not a dozen feet off. His boots were unlaced and planted wide in snowshoes of the ancient wood type. His jacket was undone, but at least he'd had the sense to wear a hat. The old man would catch his death one of these days, Micah knew. Then again, he was a hardy old nut.

"What're you doing up here?" Micah asked gently.

"I heard you were alone. You won't finish in time if you're alone."

"You shouldn't be here, Billy."

"Because my brother forbade it? That was lots of years ago. Isn't it time to let go of the past?"

Micah snorted. "Maybe I could if I knew what it was."

"Well, I'll tell you what it was," Billy said. "Your father, Dale, imagined I was coveting his wife, and there was never any truth to it. We were just friends, but he was a jealous man. Know what set him off? I cried at her funeral. Hell, someone had to. You were in shock, and Dale was angry, like she asked for that cancer. Once she was gone, he needed someone to blame, and there I was, her friend. He blamed me for that and for every other dream he'd ever had that wasn't about to come true. He said he'd shoot me on sight if I came up here again, so I didn't. How long's he been dead now?"

"Eleven years," Micah managed to say, though he was startled. He hadn't heard this story. His father hadn't been a talker.

"And we're still listening to him, you and me?" Billy asked. "Well hell, you're not. You bring me wood. You bring me clothes. You bring me food. And you say I can't help here?"

Micah did all those things. He had a soft spot in his heart for his uncle. Billy had taught him much of what he knew—had taught him quietly behind the back of the tough boss, Billy's older brother. Micah could remember laughing with Billy. He had never laughed with his father. Dale Smith had been a stern, impatient man.

"I didn't say you couldn't help here," Micah said. "*He* did."

"But he's dead, Micah. This all's yours now, and you'd've done fine if your woman had been here, but she isn't. You've told everyone in town that you don't need help, just like Dale did. But you're never gonna get it done in time for first run if you don't let someone help. In case you've forgotten, Nephew, I've done this before."

"Not with tubing."

"So show me. I can learn. Sugaring was my life for more years than I can count. If you don't want anyone in town knowing I'm here, I won't tell. But let me help. I don't have many years left. I want to do it again before I die."

While Micah let one part of the past go and Griffin chased down another, Cassie called the Chicago office of Weymarr, Higgins, and Hack and asked for Jonathan Fitzgerald. His name was the one on the letter that Heather had stashed in her knapsack.

When Jonathan Fitzgerald picked up the phone, she said, "Mr. Fitzgerald, my name is Cassandra Byrnes. I'm a lawyer, and I'm calling on behalf of a client who needs your help." She was hoping that the DiCenzas hadn't already gotten to Jonathan Fitzgerald.

"What's the problem?" he asked in a pleasant tone.

"My client had a baby a while back. You helped arrange a private adoption. She wants to locate the child, and we're wondering if you kept records and would have that information."

"I can't give out adoption information. There are strict laws governing confidentiality. You'd have to file a petition stating a pressing reason for wanting the information—such as a medical condition."

"My client has been accused of murder. It could be that DNA tests on the child will show a relationship between my client and the deceased that could be key to my client's defense."

"How far are we talking?"

"Fourteen and a half years."

"The client's name?"

"Heather Malone," Cassie said.

There was a pause on the other end, then a surprised "The same Heather Malone?"

Cassie was relieved. His surprise was genuine. "The same."

"I was wondering, when I heard it on the news."

"I was afraid the DiCenza family reached you before I did."

"I doubt they know about me."

"Then you must have a very good memory."

"Not always. I used to handle a lot of these cases. Most of them were easy. Heather had more trouble than some of the others."

"Trouble?"

"Giving up the child. I felt bad for her. Most of the girls who come to me have someone with them—friend, parent, probation officer—but she was alone."

"Would you have thought she was capable of murder?"

"No, nor extortion." Before Cassie could ask, he explained, "I read about that in the paper. No, the Heather Malone who came to me had trouble taking money at all. Living expenses, hospital costs—she would have paid for everything herself if I hadn't told her that this was how private adoptions worked. I gave her money to rent a room. When the child was born early, Heather returned the money she didn't use. Doesn't sound like a gold digger to me."

"Would you testify to that?"

"I would."

"But you won't help me locate the child?"

"I can't. The law forbids it. But if you can come up with evidence to show the need for it, I'll go to the judge myself."

When Griffin arrived at Aidan Greene's house, the sight of two cars in the driveway of the small brick home on a modest treelined street told him that Aidan hadn't yet left for work.

Griffin parked, went up the front steps, and knocked on the door, which was opened by a woman close to his age. She had a young child on her hip and another in her belly. She seemed friendly, trusting, not wary at all.

"I'm looking for Aidan Greene," he said with his most amiable smile. "My name is Griffin Hughes. We have a mutual friend."

She smiled. "You do?" She turned her head. "*Aidan?*" She faced Griffin again. "Are you from California?"

"No, but my friend is." He glanced at her belly. "Is this your second?"

"Third," she said good-naturedly as her husband came up from behind. She tipped her head back. "Honey, this is Griffin Hughes. He knows friends of yours in California."

Aidan Greene was Griffin's height, though a bit heavier. Beneath short blond hair he had fair skin and a furrowed brow. One look at Griffin, and the furrows deepened. "The bath's ready for Jessie," he told her. "Want to take her in while Griffin and I talk?"

His wife smiled at Griffin and left.

"Who's our mutual friend?" Aidan asked coldly.

"Lisa."

He started to close the door.

Putting a foot in the way, Griffin kept his voice low. "Please hear me out. My friend is actually Heather. She's made a good life for herself in New Hampshire. Something doesn't add up."

Aidan pushed at the door. "You're trespassing. Get your foot out of the way, or I'll call the cops."

"If you do that, I'll have to tell them and the papers why I'm here. And if the Sacramento *Bee* gets wind of it, they may come running up here, too. It took us a while to find you. Someone went to the effort of erasing the tracks in the snow, so to speak."

Aidan wasn't amused. "Why are you here? How'd you get my name? What do you want from me?"

"Heather gave me your name, which is why I'm here, and as for what I want from you, I have no idea. She wouldn't say. She won't say much of anything, which means that she'll be returned to Sacramento and put on trial for murder."

"That's not my worry."

"I can understand that. But right now there are a whole lot of people in New Hampshire who are worried." He pulled photos from his pocket and showed Aidan the first. "Here's Heather. This was taken last summer. That's Micah with her. She's worried that Micah won't love her if he knows the truth, and he's worried because he needs her in his life and now she's gone."

Griffin turned to the second photo. "Here's Heather with the girls. That's Missy on the left and Star on the right. Missy's seven. Star is five. Their biological mother died when Star was two months old. Heather's the only mother they know. She's a good mother."

Griffin brought up the last photo. "Here she is with her friends. Cassie's a lawyer. Poppy's been in a wheelchair since a snowmobile accident twelve years ago. Heather was a major source of support during her recovery. She's gentle and quiet but always upbeat and smiling. She reminds me of your wife, which raises the issue of your relationship with Heather. What were you to her?"

"I don't know Heather."

"Lisa, then. Were you her lover?"

Aidan shook his head. "I was not involved with Lisa."

"But Rob was, and you were his best friend. Tell me something."

"Tell you what? That she didn't do it? I didn't see anything."

"That's what you told the police. But then you left Sacramento and severed ties with the DiCenzas, and I'm thinking that you didn't want to have to remember them."

"Didn't want to have to be *beholden* to them is more like it," Aidan scoffed. "Do you know what that family's like? Do you know the power they wield? Charlie DiCenza can make you or break you. One phone call, and he can get you fired from your job and blacklisted for sins you never considered, much less committed."

"Did you know that Rob beat Lisa?" Griffin asked.

Aidan said nothing.

"We have doctors who'll testify to it," Griffin said. "Do you think she deliberately ran him down?"

"I have no idea. I gotta get to work."

"I know. I got here as early as I could. By the way, I think it's pretty neat, what you do. Did you get the counseling degree after you left California?"

Aidan nodded.

"And before that you worked for the DiCenza Foundation. Put those two things together, and I'd say you're a decent person. I'm surprised what happened with Rob and Lisa isn't eating you alive."

Aidan suddenly looked like it was.

"Was it premeditated?" Griffin prodded. "No one will tell us. No one will talk. Here's a woman who has made something of her life, and all that's about to go down the tubes because a family wants revenge. When does it end? With her execution, for God's sake?"

"It wasn't premeditated," Aidan said, and closed his mouth.

"Don't stop there," Griffin warned, "unless they have their claws in you still. Is that it? Did the DiCenzas get you your current job?"

"No." His back was suddenly solid. Griffin had pushed the right button. It had PRIDE written all over it. "They have *nothing* to do with my job or my home or my wife or my kids. Everything I have now I've earned myself, and I've done it in spite of having to live with the memories of that night. I became a school counselor to help kids because I couldn't help Lisa. She got a raw deal."

"You say it in the past tense," Griffin said, "but it's not over. It may just be starting for Heather. We need to know what happened that night. Your name is the only piece of information she's given us. She hasn't even admitted to being Lisa. You're the connection. So here's your chance for redemption. Talk to me, Aidan."

It had been arrogant of Griffin to think he could get through to Aidan. Aidan hadn't responded to the pitch he'd made at the door, nor the one he'd made later in the school corridor, nor the one he'd made in the parking lot when Aidan returned to his car after work.

Discouraged, Griffin took an evening plane back to Manchester and drove back to Poppy's.

Poppy heard Victoria first. The cat was sitting on the bed facing the door, meowing in the dark as stocking feet padded down the hall. Seconds later Griffin was sitting on the side of the bed. Poppy stared at him. "What time is it?" she whispered.

"Two."

"How did it go?" she asked.

"Lousy. I'm exhausted, so if you want sex, babe, you're out of luck. I just want to sleep with you, Poppy. Can I do that?"

She did want sex. She had been thinking about him all day, wanting to know that what they'd done was real, wanting to hear him say that he had been satisfied in spite of her limitations and that he wanted more. But life was about more than sex, and he was clearly upset. The fact that he had come to her touched her deeply.

Feeling oddly satisfied, nearly as pleased as if he had fallen on her in lust, she maneuvered herself back and raised the quilt.

Griffin didn't sleep for more than four hours. His mind was filled with wayward little thoughts that gave him a buzz. He needed to be up on his feet doing something distracting. He needed to do something that was physical, practical, and positive. Leaving Poppy in bed, he arrived at Micah's just as the girls were going off with Camille for the day. Micah was tapping. Griffin wanted in.

Billy Farraway was already there. He sat on the tailgate of Micah's truck, looking for all the world like he was going to work. Griffin might have asked about that if another truck hadn't come down the drive. Police officer Pete Duffy emerged from its cab at the same time Micah came out of the house.

Both men stopped and stared at each other.

Micah said, "I thought I told you not to come."

"That was last weekend," Pete replied. "This is this weekend. Time's running short. My guess is the sap'll be running Monday or Tuesday. I'm off work for three days. I want to help."

"Do the feds know you're here?"

"No," Pete snapped. "This is my business, not theirs. I don't work for them. The only reason I came here with them that morning was because Willie Jake told me to, and I do work for him."

"Does he know you're here?" Micah asked.

Pete didn't blink. "Sure does. He has no problem with it. You're the only one who has a problem. So you can stand there and call me a traitor, or you can take me up on my offer. If you have Billy and Griffin, my being here makes four. That's two teams. It means twice as much work gets done."

"He's right, Micah," Billy said.

Micah shot the old man a dark look and turned to Griffin. "You want to put in your two bits?"

Griffin shook his head. "I just need to work."

They worked Saturday and Sunday, twelve hours each day. Griffin had never been more tired in his life, but there was satisfaction along with the fatigue. By Monday noon the south-facing slope—two thirds of the sugar bush—had been tapped and was ready to go.

In another world Griffin might have taken the rest of the day off. Mother Nature, though, was closing in fast. There were still more than a dozen acres to tap. But he needed an hour to himself, he told Micah. No, two hours. He promised to be back then.

While he drove, he called Aidan Greene's office and left a message on the answering machine. Mother Nature wasn't the only one closing in fast; so, Cassie said, was the attorney general of California.

"Aidan, it's Griffin Hughes. I'm hoping you've thought about what we discussed. You have my number. Call anytime." He punched off just as he pulled up at Poppy's.

Poppy was at her phone bank, looking out at the lake,

when she heard the sound of Buck's old rattletrap. A minute later Griffin came in the front door. His cheeks were ruddy, his eyes excited.

"We're nearly done," he said. "Another day, and that's it."

Poppy smiled. "That's nice."

He looked down the hall to the bedroom. "I thought maybe . . ."

"Maybe what?" She wasn't making it easy.

He sighed. "I thought maybe you'd let me hold you."

"You did that Friday night for all of four hours, and you haven't been here since then. That doesn't say much for what we had."

"What did we have?"

"Great sex."

"Great sex? I'd say there was more. I'd say there was love. I said I loved you. You didn't want to hear that. Tell me why."

"I'm not ready. It's too soon. You haven't known me long enough to think you love me."

"I've spent a long time looking for the right woman," he replied, looking hurt. "I think I know what I want. I think you do, too, only you're afraid to go after it."

"Why am I afraid?" she asked, unable to say the words herself.

"Because you're disabled. Because you think that has to matter to me, and you're afraid of rejection. You're afraid that I'll get tired of being with someone who can't do the things I can."

Keeping up with him wasn't her greatest worry. "There's still a lot that you don't know about me."

"Well, that would be the accident," he said. Tossing his jacket on the sofa, he pulled up a chair. "So tell me about it."

She didn't want to. But Griffin wasn't about to let this go. "I was in the hospital for eight weeks. I was in a coma for the first one. Then I woke up and learned what had happened. It was difficult."

He frowned. Not being able to move? she imagined him thinking.

"Knowing Perry was dead," she corrected. "He'd been buried by then, and everyone tried to gloss over it and tell me how lucky I was, but it took me a while to see that. They got me up and around. The last few weeks of the eight I was in a rehab center."

He was patient. "What do you remember of the accident?"

"Not much. It was a horrible night."

"There was a party with drinking." His tone urged her to go on.

But she was done. She didn't want to think about this. She was paying the price of irresponsibility by living in a wheelchair. She didn't owe Griffin further penance.

He looked at her. "When I first got back here after Heather's arrest, I said that you trusted me on some level. You argued, but I believed it then, and I believe it now. Only, that level doesn't go as deep as I thought." He rose and went for his jacket. "You and Heather are two peas in a pod. Neither one of you trusts that someone can know everything about you and still love you."

"What do you want me to say?" she cried.

He shrugged. "I have to get back," he said, and left.

Chapter Eight

First thing Tuesday morning the sap started to flow. Micah saw the telltale slide of liquid down the tubing. He spent the morning tapping trees on the north-facing slopes. There was no sap flow there, probably wouldn't be for a week. Still, spring was on its way.

He wished Heather were there. She had loved this. He wished the girls were there right then, too, so that they could share the excitement. Later they would be there. Poppy would bring them from school, and they would help. Sugar making was a family affair.

At least it used to be. And now? He and Billy were family, but Griffin was not. Nor was Pete, though he had surely proved himself a friend. With Pete back being a cop today, Billy and Griffin were a team, while Micah worked alone.

He would have liked to team up with a son. He had told Heather that. But in the absence of a son, he did have his trees. They would be here for him whether the girls married, Heather was convicted, or old Billy died. He had raised them and nurtured them. He had protected them until they were mature enough to tap, and he had staked them when they needed support.

They were his children. He took pride in their performance now.

Poppy got the call shortly after noon and began making calls of her own. She didn't have to mince words. "Sap's running" was all she had to say, and the townsfolk took it from there. They hung up the phone and rushed to the sugarhouse, laden with food and drink to feed the sugar maker, his assistants, and as many visitors as chose to drop by. At least that was the way it had been in the past. This time the reception Poppy got was only lukewarm.

"Oh?" one said. "Well, it's time, I guess."

From another, "I hope it's a good year. He's had a rough spell."

Poppy's mother was the only one who expressed any of the usual excitement. But then Maida was a cider maker. She knew what it was to approach the finish line with the fruit of one's labor. She also loved to cook.

"I'm already in the kitchen," she told Poppy. "Let me make a few more things. Midafternoon I'll be at Micah's."

"Why don't I come get you?" Poppy suggested. "Can you be ready by three?"

"I surely can," Maida promised, and she was. Poppy picked up the girls from school first. She had barely pulled up in front of her mother's handsome fieldstone home when Maida came out. She deposited one wicker basket of foil packs in the back of the Blazer, ran back in for a second, then a third.

Poppy pulled up to the sugarhouse. Steam billowed from the cupola, drifting up through the tops of the trees and into the sky over town. Even more than Poppy's phone calls, the steam should have been a rallying cry. Cars should have been coming down Micah's drive, disgorging townsfolk.

This year there were no cars arriving other than Poppy's. She parked beside Griffin's truck and let the girls out. They bolted inside as Maida and Poppy went around to the back to get the food, which they would finish preparing in Heather's kitchen.

Inside the sugarhouse, Griffin was the grunt man. His job was to fire up the arch under the evaporator pan and to restack wood as the pile was depleted. Missy and Star helped with the stacking, running one log at a time from the woodpile to the pallet by the arch. Early on, they threw their jackets aside because the sugarhouse was warm. It was also moist; Missy's hair grew curlier and curlier.

Griffin teased her. "You are just growing more and more and more hair," he said. "Did you eat something special for breakfast?"

Missy shook her head and did a little dance around the room. Star was quieter, staying close to his side. From time to time she reached into his coat pocket, pulled out a chocolate kiss, and unwrapped it. He had made sure that the ones in his pockets had nuts.

Micah was the sugar maker. He was the maestro, and the process wasn't simple at all. He explained it in a quiet voice as he monitored, shifted, directed, and scooped. "This valve allows sap to flow in from the tank outside. Once it comes in, it goes first through the reverse osmosis machine. That takes out a lot of the water. From there it goes to the back flue. Then it comes into the back pan and is brought to a boil." He moved the liquid forward with a large metal scoop. "This next pan, the middle one of the three, is smaller than the back one because the sap's already starting to condense."

"Can I taste?" Missy asked.

"Not yet," Micah said. "But soon." He moved more sap along. "The front pan is the last stage. This is where sap turns into syrup."

"How do you know when that happens?" Griffin asked.

"You hear it," Billy put in.

Micah explained, "There's a subtle change in the bubbling. If you don't hear it, you can tell from the thermometer in here. Sap changes to syrup when it reaches seven degrees above boiling."

"Something smells wonderful," came a voice from the door. It was Lily Kipling, followed closely by her husband and Charlie Owens. When they took off their coats and looked ready to stay, Griffin left the girls in their care and went down to the house.

Micah liked talking about what he did. He felt competent and strong. With the arrival of guests, though, his attention was thrown off. Friends and neighbors stopping by at the first sign of sugar steam was the way in Lake Henry. This year he would rather have done without their visit. Oh, he needed Billy and Griffin—they did the peripherals while he handled the sap. He also didn't mind it when Maida brought food and drink up from the house. And he surely didn't mind Poppy coming up. She was practically family.

He could have done without Lily, John, and Charlie, though. They reminded him of the crowds that used to come with the first sap and how different it was this year. Worse, Charlie knew it, too, and tried to be solicitous.

"What needs to be done?" he asked, rubbing his hands together.

"I'm set," Micah answered, eyes on the bubbling gold in the pan.

"Did you finish puttin' in spiles?"

"No. I'll do it mornings. Can't boil until afternoon, anyway."

"I can spare a boy or two if you need them," Charlie offered.

"I'm fine," Micah said, setting his jaw. Truth was, he felt like a fool in the eyes of the town, what with Heather turning out to be someone else and his not knowing a thing. She might as well have cheated on him. He felt humiliated.

Poppy was sitting on Micah's old sofa when Griffin came down the hall from the kitchen. She smiled when he came in.

He smiled back. "Your mom's busy as a bee back there. I thought you'd be helping. Are you okay?"

She wasn't sure. She felt . . . blue. But she nodded anyway and gestured for Griffin to come close. When he hunkered down, she bent forward and put her nose to his flannel shirt. "Mmmm. Maple sugar. It's an insidious smell. How's it going up there?"

"Your sister came."

Lily. *Mommy-to-be*. "She's pregnant, only no one's supposed to know yet, so don't say anything."

"I won't. Thanks for telling me. A new baby's always exciting."

Poppy nodded. She laced her fingers in her lap.

"Something is wrong," he said, still on his haunches. "Are you still angry at me for what I said?"

"I should be."

"Why? Because I love you? That's crazy. Let's cut to the chase." Everything about him gentled then, from his eyes to his voice to the hands he placed on either side of her face. "I know about the accident, Poppy. I *know* about it. Imagine the worst, and I know it. If you think I'll find out about it later and hate you, you're wrong."

Poppy could barely breathe. She couldn't speak.

"It's a matter of forgiveness," Griffin went on. "You have it, but it's not even needed. Even when I dream up the worst-case scenario, I don't see any malice on your part in what happened that night."

Poppy was silent. No, no malice, she thought, just a gross irresponsibility that had caused a person's death.

"The problem isn't really about me. You don't need me to forgive you for what happened that night. You need to forgive yourself."

"What do you want me to do?" she whispered. But he wasn't giving her the answer she needed. He couldn't. She knew that.

Instead, quietly, he said, "Let me come home to you at night. I'll work here with Micah as long as he needs me. But I don't want Little Bear late at night. I want you."

She put her fingers to his mouth. He was a remarkable man, seemingly hers for the taking, but she didn't deserve him. That said, she wasn't about to deny his request. She might be guilty of things she hadn't ever spoken aloud, but she wasn't stupid.

Griffin was at the sugarhouse until midnight that night, until past eleven on Wednesday, and until midnight again on Thursday. For all those years of opening tins of maple syrup and carelessly pouring it on pancakes, he had never imagined the work that went into the making. Once the sap became syrup, it had to be filtered to remove the tiniest specks of grit. Bottling immediately followed; then everything that had been used in the sugarhouse had to be cleaned.

By the time he got to Poppy's each night, he was exhausted. Truth be told, he couldn't have made it to Little Bear if his life had depended on it. The days were just too exhausting. He was bone-tired when he climbed into bed beside Poppy, and he was up with first light to go back and help Micah.

Come Saturday morning, when Griffin and Poppy awoke to a light drizzle, he would have given anything just to stay in bed with her. But sugar maples knew nothing about weekends. Nor did they care about rain. When the sap ran, it ran, and it had to be processed. Besides, there were still trees to tap. With a little luck they would finish the last of the slopes before noon. That in itself was cause for showing up to work.

An even better cause presented itself that day. As they were coming down from the sugar bush for lunch, a nondescript car pulled in. Griffin recognized the man behind the wheel as Aidan Greene.

Micah's heart pounded as Aidan approached, though Aidan wasn't what Micah had expected. Micah had expected power. He had expected arrogance and savvy. This man was dressed well enough, but nothing about him suggested privilege. He looked tired and wan. Hollow. Even apprehensive.

Griffin met him halfway and extended a hand. "I'd have picked you up at the airport if you'd called."

"I didn't know I was coming," Aidan said. "Didn't know if I'd make it all the way here. A guy in the general store in town told me where you were." He shot Micah a glance.

Micah couldn't get himself to go forward. Greene was a real-life figure from Heather's past. If Micah acknowledged his existence, he had to detest the fact that the man had taken this long to speak up.

"That surly guy is Micah," Griffin advised. "He's having trouble with all this, so if he lacks graciousness, we have to forgive him. Can we go inside?" he asked Micah.

Micah nodded. They went in through the kitchen, where

Poppy was at the table with the girls. They had just finished lunch. A platter of sandwiches awaited the men.

Micah couldn't eat a thing, and he told Poppy as much with a look. Griffin and Aidan followed him through the kitchen. He heard Poppy offer them food, heard them refuse everything but coffee. Micah didn't offer anyone a seat in the living room. He stood against the wall by the window, folded his arms, and waited.

Aidan was draping his coat on a chair. He looked up, seeming relieved when Poppy wheeled in with coffee. "Headache," he murmured as he reached for the coffee and took several desperate sips. Poppy parked near the sofa, clearly staying. Micah figured she had a right. After the girls and him, she was the one most deeply affected by Heather's secret past.

Griffin said to Aidan, "You were determined not to talk when I was in Minneapolis. What changed your mind?"

"You made a remark about my becoming a counselor, and you were right. I am a do-gooder, always was. That's why Rob loved having me around. Teaming up with me helped his image."

"Why did he need help?" Griffin asked. "He was a DiCenza. The family is famously charitable."

Aidan shot him a dry look. "When you have as much money as the DiCenzas, you have to do something with it or you end up giving it to Uncle Sam. Charlie DiCenza would choke to death before he did that. The DiCenza Foundation was created primarily as a tax deduction. The charitable image was a side benefit."

"Did you know all this back then?"

"Yes. We all did. But when you're young, you think you can jump on the bandwagon of a powerful entity and use it for your own ends. You don't realize that they've sunk their teeth into you until it's too late to shake them off. By then they own you."

"You shook them off."

"Not back then. I have a law degree. I got it straight from college. I had it the whole time the business with Rob and Lisa was going on. Rob was my friend, so I felt a loyalty to him, and the old man had that power. I really thought he was going to be elected Vice President, in which case there might be a nice position for me in the White House. I had this illusion that I could milk him for that and then use the position to do some good. I was naïve."

"How so?" Griffin asked.

"Because I kept my mouth shut about Lisa and Rob, I'd in essence perjured myself." He waved a hand. "Oh, it wasn't official, but it was there in my mind. I'd sold out. I was doing small-time legal stuff for the DiCenza Foundation, and suddenly I couldn't stomach it. I felt like a fraud. So I dropped out. Resurfacing as a counselor felt better."

Micah was feeling antsy. He had work to do. "Well, you're just a model citizen," he said mockingly. "A bad guy gone good."

Aidan stared at him. "I try."

"Now try something for Heather's sake. Try the truth."

"She loved Rob DiCenza," Aidan said.

That hurt. Micah knew Aidan had meant for it to. He backed off.

Griffin asked Aidan, "Did Rob love her?"

"Rob wasn't capable of love as you and I know it. He was raised in a family where love was bartered—you do this for me, I do this for you. Nothing was pure. Lisa's love was pure."

"Did she set her sights on him, like the papers said?" Griffin asked.

"No. She wasn't sophisticated or self-confident enough. He was the one who went after her, not the other way around. She worked for the caterer that the DiCenza family used. They were always having parties, so she was over there twice a month. Rob was probably initially attracted to her because she was poor. It drove Charlie nuts."

"Did you know that Rob knocked her around?" Griffin asked.

Aidan studied his coffee. "He said she mouthed off. That she deserved what she got."

"What about the pregnancy?"

Aidan looked away. "When she told him about it, he said that she was trying to trap him, that it wasn't his, that he'd pay for an abortion out of the goodness of his heart, but only because he liked her."

"Did she agree to get the abortion?"

"No. That was the problem. She kept hoping he'd soften and decide that he wanted the baby, too. She told me about it, thinking I could convince him that it wouldn't be so bad having the baby."

"Did you try?"

"There was no point. I knew how he felt. Like I said, Rob was incapable of love. So I told her she could do better. I told her to leave town, have the baby, and find another guy."

Poppy said quietly, "In some regards, that's what she did."

"Except that something happened in the just-leave-town stage," Griffin said. "We're missing a page." He looked at Aidan. "Were you there that night?"

Aidan stood straighter. "I was. But I wasn't in the men's room."

The telling of the story took five minutes and left Micah with two problems. The first was that he wouldn't believe Aidan until Heather confirmed what the man said, and Heather wasn't talking. The second was more immediate. Aidan had no sooner finished speaking when Micah noticed a ripple in the cloth that covered the table and reached the floor. He crossed the room, raised the fabric, and lifted out Star. "You're not supposed to be here," he scolded, but totally without anger.

"I want Momma," the little girl said.

He held her cheek to his shoulder. "We're working on getting her back. That's what this is about." He looked around the room, searching out other little hiding places. "Where's your sister?"

"In the clubhouse. She doesn't want that man here."

Micah headed for the hall. "Call Cassie," he told Griffin, and holding Star, went to the girls' bedroom. The closet door was ajar.

"Come out here, Missy."

"No," said a muted voice.

He opened the door. Blankets were draped off hooks, so he couldn't see Missy, but he heard her again.

"*You* can come in, but not that man and not Heather," she said.

Micah squatted down, settling Star on his knee. "Why not Heather?"

"She isn't in our family anymore."

"Why not?"

"Because I don't like that man."

Micah knew what she was trying to say. Aidan represented a part of Heather that was frightening to them.

"Come out here," he coaxed. "It's just me and Star."

"And Poppy and Griffin. I don't like him, either."

"I do," said Star.

Missy stuck her head out from between the blankets.

"That's because you like chocolate, but you're too little to see what I see."

"What do you see?" Micah asked.

"That he's trying to take Poppy away from us, just like someone took Heather and someone took Mommy."

"He's not doing that. What's going on isn't about taking away. It's about adding. Adding Griffin to Poppy. Adding Heather to us."

Missy's eyes were stormy. "I don't need Heather."

"I thought you loved her," Micah said.

Star looked up at him. "*I* do. You do, too, don't you?"

"Micah," Poppy called from the door. "Cassie wants us to come."

He rose, taking Star up again. "I can't go. The girls and I have sap to boil." Skirting the wheelchair, he set off for the kitchen. Billy was there, eating a sandwich. Micah went through the back hall and had a hand on the door when Griffin's voice stopped him.

"We have to meet with Heather. Aidan's coming."

Micah looked back. "Be my guest."

Poppy wheeled around Griffin. "You have to be there, Micah," she said. "It's important."

Micah wished she was right. But he'd been there before, and Heather hadn't talked. So what good was he on that score? "I have to work, Poppy. Sap's running. If I don't do this, who will?"

"Me," said Billy, coming up from behind Griffin. "Let me use your phone, and I'll get help. I'm not without friends in this town."

Poppy wheeled close and said with quiet urgency, "How can you be angry, after what Aidan said? We're so close. Cassie needs to hear the story from Heather. Don't you?"

He did. That was all he'd wanted for days.

"Seeing Aidan could make it happen," Poppy went on. "But if you're not there, Heather might not care. She loves you, Micah. If ever she needed you, now's the time." She paused for a breath, then whispered, "Heather's already afraid she's lost you, because you haven't been to see her. Can't you forgive her?"

He was spared having to answer by Star. "I helped Poppy make the sandwiches, and there's tuna there. Momma loves tuna. Maybe if you bring her one, she'll think of me."

The room was small for five people, but Cassie insisted that all five were vital to Heather's defense, so the guard showed them in. Micah stayed in the background, telling himself that he was only there for Star's sake—until the door opened and Heather came in. When her eyes went right to his, he knew he was lying to himself. His heart ached as it had done when she had first been taken away.

Then Heather saw Aidan, and what little color she had drained away. She looked frantically at Cassie, who went to her, took her hands, and spoke softly. "I finally have a workable argument," she said. "With Aidan testifying about the abuse, we can make a case that you feared for your life."

Heather sent Aidan a skeptical look.

"The DiCenza family prides itself on its image," Cassie continued. "They've spoken long and hard about how terrible you are, and their words have gone unchallenged because you haven't been there to speak for yourself. Things will be different if you decide to talk. They'll hate what you say, and they won't want you quoted in the press. They'll want this settled quickly and quietly."

Heather glanced at Aidan again and whispered, "Why now?"

The room was small. Her whisper carried.

Aidan answered, "Because they're abusers—and not only physically. They abuse power, and that's not right. You suffered. I know. I drove you to the hospital—twice. And I did tell the old man. He said he was going to forget I said it and that I'd best do the same."

"And you did!" Micah charged. "You kept your damned mouth shut when they accused her of murder!"

"She was gone," Aidan argued. "There was no trial. She escaped. She made a better life. My crime wasn't in keeping quiet then; it was in letting things go so far now. I'll have to live with that. But it's not too late to change the outcome."

Cassie pressed her case. "And then there's the child." Heather's eyes flew to Micah. "Rob's mother won't want word coming out that her son wanted to abort his own child."

"He said it wasn't his," Heather said in a whisper.

"Tests can prove that it was. We can find her, Heather."

"She'll hate me for what I did."

"*No one* hates you for what you did then. But your silence—this silence—is inexcusable. Anything else we can forgive."

Again Heather's eyes went to Micah. Micah didn't hear much of what Cassie said next. He was too busy remembering all that had been good about his life with Heather, all that he still wanted. Yes, he did want it, especially when she looked at him the way she was looking now, as though he was the center of her universe, as though his love was the only thing she had ever truly wanted.

Suddenly the wall he leaned against was cold and hard. Moving away from it, he wrapped his hands around her neck and tipped her chin up with both thumbs. "Tell me," he said. "In your words."

She lingered a minute, searching his face. She closed her

hands on his wrists and held tight. The words came in a woeful rush.

"I didn't want to date him. I mean, I *did* because someone like me dating someone like him was a dream come true, but I knew it couldn't work. We were too different. He kept saying it was all right, that he loved me, that we needed to keep our relationship secret until just the right time, and then he'd tell the world."

"But he hit you," Micah said.

"When he drank. He always apologized for the drink—and for the hitting. Then I got pregnant, and things fell apart. He was furious." Her voice fell to a whisper. "I wanted the baby so much. I didn't demand he marry me. I just wanted him to help me keep the baby."

"Were you arguing about the baby that night?"

"I wasn't going to say anything. I was working. But he kept seeking me out and following me around, and he kept drinking. He started calling me names, loudly, so I finally went off with him to try to calm him down. He wanted to know if I'd aborted the baby yet, and when I said I hadn't, he said he'd do it for me."

Micah felt sick. "Do it?"

"Kick me. He said he could kick the baby out, and he started pushing me. When I turned and ran, he followed."

Micah could see the pain in her eyes. "Then what happened?"

Her eyes filled with tears. "I believed he would kick me and kill the baby. So I ran between the cars on the field and got to my own because I had to get away. I started to drive, and it was dark. I got to an open part of the field, and I remember thinking I was almost free, so I went faster. I had no idea he'd race out in front of the car." She had started to shake. "I didn't know he was dead."

"But you ran."

"He was a DiCenza. He could have ended up with a concussion, and the family would have come after me. They'd have sent me to prison and taken my baby. Yes, I ran, and when I learned that he was dead, I kept running. It nearly killed me to give the baby up, but I wanted her to be safe. Then I came to Lake Henry and found you and the girls, and I just pushed all of that unhappiness out of my mind. When you do that, you can pretend it never happened."

Micah looked at Aidan. "Is what she said consistent with what you witnessed?"

Aidan nodded. "He was drunk. He threatened her."

Cassie asked, "And you'll testify to that?"

"Yes."

Heather's hands tightened on Micah's wrists. "I don't want to go back there. You don't know the power they have."

No, Micah didn't. He had been privileged to spend his life with more decent people than the DiCenzas. Heather would probably have to return to California, and God knew what faced her there. He did know one thing, though. When she went, she wouldn't be alone.

Poppy wanted to celebrate. She knew that Cassie still had to get Heather the best possible deal, and then there was the child. They had to locate her if the threat of DNA testing was to hold water. But that afternoon they had come so much further than they previously had been that Poppy felt giddy. She felt optimistic. She felt brave.

When she returned to the house, she still had energy to spare, so she went to the exercise room and wheeled over to the wall. She took the braces down, held them, turned them.

Then she heard the sound of a snowmobile on the lake and went to the wall of windows. A headlight cut through the fast-fading day. She watched the helmeted driver park the machine, knowing exactly who it was. Dropping the braces, she wheeled out to the main room and opened the deck door to let him in.

Removing the helmet, Griffin grinned. "Hey."

She grinned back, helpless to resist. "Hey, yourself."

"We did good today. So I'm here to take you for a ride."

She knew what he was feeling. There was a light-headedness that came with the sudden easing of a weight. But she didn't do snowmobiles anymore. "Maybe another time," she said.

"I want to take you to Little Bear."

"It's raining," she tried.

"Not now it isn't. It's barely misting. Billy told me to use his snowmobile, so I thought we'd do dinner out there. I picked up chili at Charlie's. You love Charlie's chili."

Poppy eyed the machine. "I can't go on that."

"Is it a matter of distrust?"

"No. Bad memories."

"Come on, Poppy," Griffin coaxed. "It was stormy that night. What happened had nothing to do with booze. It could have happened to the best of drivers."

Poppy's said, "I don't have any more right to go out on a snowmobile than I have to walk or get married or have kids."

"So sin again," he said, and before she knew what he was up to, he had her in her parka and had lifted her in his arms.

"I don't want to do this, Griffin," she said, feeling more than a little unease. "It's getting dark. Snowmobiles scare me. I want my chair." The cold hit her face when he opened the door, but it was eased moments later when he slid a helmet over her head.

Straddling the snowmobile, he set her sidesaddle before him and pulled on his own helmet. Only then did he pause.

He raised both faceplates. "If you don't want to do this, I'll take you back inside."

If he hadn't given her the choice, Poppy might have refused him. She was an adult. She was her own person. She saw no reason why she should be railroaded into *anything*, let alone something that was emotionally disturbing for her. But emotions ran two ways. Yes, being on a snowmobile brought back memories. But she didn't want to go back inside. It was a night to celebrate. This was fitting.

Fitting barely described it. The ride out over the lake was exhilarating, dinner in front of the fire was charming, lovemaking in the afterglow was divine.

The next morning, wet snow clumped on the windows and the cabin was dark, so it was a while before they realized that they had overslept. Then Griffin bolted up and checked his watch. "Omigod. It's ten thirty. I was supposed to be at Micah's."

"I don't think you'll make it. Look outside."

Griffin hurried to the door, inched it open, peered out. His voice held awe. "Everything is frozen. Good thing we finished tapping yesterday." He shut the door tight and returned to bed.

By noon a freezing rain was falling, making the thought of a snowmobile ride even more unappealing. So they stoked the fire, ate soup from the pot, and fell back to sleep. By one they were awake again and looking outside. Ice was thick on everything in sight, and a freezing rain continued to fall. Figuring that it had to be better in another hour, they closed the door and returned to the fire.

"If you could make one wish, what would it be?" Griffin asked.

"You first."

"Five kids, three dogs, and a cat to keep the others in line. Your turn."

"Two. I'd settle for two," she said, and looked at him in surprise.

He didn't say anything, didn't tease her for blurting it out, which made her love him all the more.

Then came the craa-aack and thud of a pine limb breaking from its trunk and hitting the ground, and Poppy felt a glimmer of worry.

"If there's damage to the sugar bush in a storm like this, what happens?" Griffin asked.

When Poppy refused to say the words, he began gathering their things.

The ride back was slow. As they crossed open ice fields, the signs of damage mounted before their eyes. Trees bent and cracked. As they neared Poppy's, they saw a tree fall across her deck.

Seconds later the deck door opened, and Maida and Poppy's sisters, Lily and Rose, came out. All three stopped then and stared—not at the tree, but at Poppy and Griffin.

Chapter Nine

Griffin pulled up as close as he could behind the fallen tree, turned off the snowmobile, and lifted Poppy. What had been snow then was now a thick coat of ice. Twice he slipped and nearly fell.

Maida looked terrified. "Thank God," she cried, following along as Griffin carried Poppy inside. "Do you know how frightened I've been? I came over first thing this morning to make sure you were all right, and you were gone. Your chair was here—your chair and your car—but no you. Do you know what went through my mind?"

"She thought you were kidnapped," Rose said, materializing beside Maida as Griffin settled Poppy in her chair. "Didn't it occur to you to call one of us and let us know where you were?"

It hadn't. Poppy felt remorse. She shot Griffin a helpless look.

"There's no phone on the island," he said. "We would have

been back this morning, but I thought the going would be too rough. I'm sorry. It was my fault."

"How could you *not* know that we would worry, Poppy?" Rose said. "You don't take off overnight. You never do that. And without your chair? You've aged Mom ten years."

"I'm all right," Maida murmured.

"It was one thing when we were kids and you had to do your own thing," Rose went on. "The wilder, the better—you didn't care what Mom and Dad thought. Only you're not a child now. I thought the accident gave you some sense of responsibility."

"Apparently not," Poppy said. "I'm an adult, and I'm still irresponsible. You're a mom, and you're still small-minded."

"Poppy," Maida begged.

But Poppy was annoyed. "She's right. I don't take off overnight, but I did it this time because there was something I wanted to do badly enough to get past the idea that I didn't have a right to do it. I've lived that way for twelve years, while Rose had a good time at college and married sweet Art and had three wonderful children, and that's fine, because she deserves all those things and I don't."

"Poppy—" Lily whispered, moving toward her.

"I don't," Poppy said, but she didn't look at Lily, only at Maida. "I was driving that night. Griffin guessed it. You must have, too."

Rose gasped. "*You* were driving?"

Poppy's eyes didn't leave her mother. She had been needing to say this for twelve years, solely to see Maida's reaction. "We were up there drinking and laughing," she said, "and when it came time to go home, Perry was tanked, so I drove. I wasn't drunk. But I went too fast and lost control. We were both thrown off. I hit the ground, so I'm in a chair. Perry hit a tree, so he's in a grave."

"Do the police know this?" Rose asked, sounding horrified.

"*Rose,*" Lily scolded, and put a reassuring hand on Poppy's shoulder.

Poppy faced Rose. "I never told them. You can if you want."

"She won't," Maida told Poppy. "There's absolutely no point."

"Maida's right," Griffin said, standing behind Poppy. "What law was broken? Reckless driving? Well, maybe there was that, but how would you punish her, Rose? What would you do?"

Rose waved a hand. "I wouldn't— I didn't say—"

"Would you put her in prison?" Griffin asked. Poppy sensed his anger and loved him for it. "Would you sentence her to life in a wheelchair—oops, she's already sentenced to that. Would you sentence her to guilt? To self-flagellation? To a public flogging?"

"I am not the bad guy here," Rose protested.

"Am I?" Poppy asked her mother.

Maida's face held pain though not surprise. "No, Poppy. You're no more the bad guy than any of the rest of us."

Tears came to Poppy's eyes, and Maida moved to hug her. Before it could happen, though, another tree fell, this one with a louder crash. Then the lights went out, leaving the room in darkness.

"Oh dear," said Maida.

The phone rang. Poppy picked it up. "Hello?"

"It's Micah. Is Griffin with you?"

"He is." Her eyes found Griffin's. "What's wrong?"

"You name it. Lights out, trees down, mainline split. I need help."

A sheet of ice covered the road. Poppy watched Rose and Lily slide around in the Suburban on their way out. Maida would have done the same in her van had Griffin not been at the wheel. He was far more cautious than a native Lake Henryite would be.

Poppy was able to spend an hour making calls before the phone lines went down. She reached the people she wanted to reach, and she wasn't settling for sympathetic murmurings about tough luck.

"Here's the scoop," she said time and again. "Trees are down in the sugar bush, and the mainline is split. It can't be repaired until the trees are *off*. We need chain saws and manpower as early as possible tomorrow at Micah's. Can you be there?" When she heard hemming and hawing, she said, "It's do or die for Micah. Without the mainline, he has no sap to boil. Sugar makers have been wiped out by storms like this." When she heard buts, she said, "I seem to recall Micah fixing your roof on Christmas Day two years ago," or she reminded them of his replacing a broken window. "He didn't charge you then, so you can pay him now with this."

She wasn't taking no for an answer.

Cassie sat at her desk making notes on a pad in the light of an oil lamp. She wanted to have her thoughts organized, given that she was making calls on a Sunday rather than waiting until the workweek began. The clock was running down. The court order keeping Heather in New Hampshire expired in twelve days. Given the story that Heather had told, finding the child was a must. Cassie's first call on her cell phone would therefore be to the Chicago lawyer Jonathan Fitzgerald. Directory assistance provided his home number.

After a single ring a woman's voice said a fast "Hello?"

"Jonathan Fitzgerald, please."

There was a release of breath and a quieter "Who is this?"

"Cassie Byrnes. I'm a colleague. I'm calling from New Hampshire. I'm sorry to be calling on a Sunday—"

"He's in the hospital. He's had a heart attack. I thought you might be the doctor. We don't know whether he'll pull through."

For a stunned minute Cassie was silent. "Oh my," she finally said. "I'm sorry."

"He's in intensive care. The next few days are crucial."

As indeed they are here, Cassie thought. "I understand." She wished the woman's husband a speedy recovery, then hung up.

Her second call was to have been to the assistant attorney general in charge of the case in Sacramento. Given this newest glitch, though, she went over his head to the attorney general himself. She got his home phone number from a law school friend who worked on numerous committees with the attorney general's wife.

Cassie was hoping the attorney general would be sympathetic to Heather and her cause. But he was a man who was beholden either to the DiCenzas or to the letter of the law. "I don't know what you want from me, Ms. Byrnes," he said after she had laid out her case. "Are you admitting Heather Malone is Lisa Matlock?"

"I can't do that until I find the child. And that's easier said than done, given what I told you about the situation in Chicago."

"There are certain accepted avenues here, Ms. Byrnes. Calling me at home isn't one. Have you talked with Mr. Grinelle about this?"

Bud Grinelle was the assistant officially leading the charge. "Mr. Grinelle has been agreeable," Cassie said, "but you and I both know that he is checking with you at every step. I haven't mentioned the child to him. Did you know about her before?"

"There were allegations at the time. The family denied them."

"Tests can prove a connection. Unfortunately, with the lawyer who handled the adoption sidelined, it will take longer to find her."

"Whenever is fine."

"Not from the point of view of my client. My own resources are limited. Yours are less so. Quite frankly, I'm thinking of the child, too. She's fourteen now. That's a vulnerable age. I'd hate to see the press ferreting her out before I'm able to. You have resources that could make it happen before harm is done to the girl."

But the man wasn't thinking about the case in human terms. "You don't seem to understand," he said. "We don't need the child. You're the one who does. We have a dozen different statements, all pointing to the theory that a scorned and conniving woman ran down a good man. We have a thorough case. The core of it will be part of the governor's warrant that we present to the judge there. We're ahead of schedule. You can expect it at the end of the week."

"Thank you," Cassie said politely. "I'm sorry to have bothered you. Enjoy the rest of your weekend." She ended the call and set down the phone. Where to go now? There was only one place. Lifting the phone again, she called Griffin.

Griffin didn't get the message until the wee hours of Monday morning, which was how late he and Micah were in the sugar bush. Assessing the damage at night was hard. Micah's first concern was the lowest portion of mainline that had split under a fallen tree. Its proximity to the sugarhouse made it a final destination for the rest of the lines, which meant that it was crucial. No sap at all would make it to the sugarhouse tanks until it was fixed.

When they returned to the house, Micah made a list of the parts he needed to buy for immediate repairs, and Griffin accessed his messages. He smiled at the ones from Poppy, amusing monologues that passed on the good news that help would be at Micah's come morning. Griffin's smile faded, though, when he listened to Cassie. Moments later he left another message for Ralph Haskins. "It's crunch time on Lisa Matlock's baby," he said. "The lawyer we thought would help is in the hospital in intensive care, and the A.G. in California would be happy if the child wasn't found at all. Also, time is shorter than we thought. The governor's warrant will be on its way by the end of the week. Do what you can." He ended the call.

"Think your man can find her?" Micah asked, looking up.

"Yes. In time to keep Heather from going back to California? I don't know."

"Micah?" Camille was at the door. She had been staying with the girls while Micah and Griffin were in the woods, and she had been asleep on the living-room sofa. "Star just woke up. Should I go in?"

"I'll go," he said quietly. As he passed her, he said, "Thanks."

When his footsteps faded, Camille looked at Griffin. Clearly she had heard the message to Ralph. "If the child is found," she asked, "would that keep Heather here?"

Griffin suddenly felt tired. "I don't know, Camille. My guess is that Heather will have to go back to face the charges at some point, but if we can find the child, the deal will be better."

Camille considered that. She looked at the table. Then she approached it, took Micah's pencil, tore off a piece of paper from the pad, and wrote down something. "That's the child you want."

Griffin studied the paper, then Camille, and suddenly it made sense—the quiet concern, the surrogate grandmotherhood here, the offer of money. "What are you to Heather?"

Camille smiled sadly. "Not her mother. That would have been too easy. I'm her aunt. Her mother was my sister. She died years ago." Camille studied her hands; then her eyes came up. "Would you like some tea?" She answered herself. "I'd like some tea." She went to the stove and put a kettle on to boil.

"Were you the older or the younger?" Griffin asked.

"Older. By four years. We were born in Eastern Europe in a small town, and after our parents died, we came here looking for a better life. I wanted to settle in a small town like the one we had left. Stacia—short for Anastasia—wanted excitement and glamour."

"Hollywood?"

Camille nodded. "She had no acting ability. I could never tell her that, of course. She had her dream. Somewhere along the line she met Harlan Matlock, who was a tortured soul." The kettle whistled; she took tea bags from the cupboard. "They went north to Sacramento and settled down, at least as much as my sister ever could. She was pregnant, but that didn't seem to help. She was restless. She needed to be on the move, only she didn't have the slightest idea where she wanted to go. She disappeared when Lisa was five." Camille poured the tea.

"Where did you come in?"

She set an earthenware mug in front of him. "The more appropriate question would be *when* did I come in, and the answer is, Too late. My sister stopped calling me somewhere between Hollywood and Sacramento. I used to dial information from time to time to see if there was a phone listing.

Whenever I got one, I called it. Harlan would answer and say Stacia was out. Then he would tell me not to call again or try to visit. He said Stacia didn't want it."

"Why is that?"

Camille sipped from her mug. "When we first came to this country, we had lofty dreams. Hers were always more so than mine. I found a lovely place here in Lake Henry. I found work and friends. There is nothing lofty about my life here, but I've been happy. Stacia was never happy. Her life was a disappointment to her. She would have been embarrassed to have me see it."

Camille continued. "I didn't learn of her death until months afterward, when I made one of those chance calls. Lisa was eight at the time. Harlan said she was fine, but I wanted to see for myself, so I flew out there. I waited at the schoolyard." She chuckled softly. "I recognized her right away. She was the image of Stacia."

"Did you talk?" Griffin asked.

"For a bit. I told her who I was. I gave her pictures that I had. I gave her my address and my phone number. I told her if she ever needed help—with anything—she should call me."

"Did she ever call?"

"Not until after the accident. She told me about the baby, so I knew where the baby was born, and we talked about her coming to Lake Henry. I didn't know she would actually do it until she arrived. She showed up one day and signed on with Charlie. We've led our own lives. It was safer that way, and our relationship has evolved naturally, as friends. No one in town suspects anything more."

Quietly Griffin asked, "Not even Micah?"

She answered in kind, little more than a whisper. "Not even Micah. If he's going to know, she'll be the one to tell him."

Griffin studied the name on the paper. "How did you get this?"

"I was at the hospital the day the baby was picked up by her adoptive family. If you're in the right place at the right time, you hear the right things. I was, and I did. I interpreted that to mean that I was meant to keep an eye on the child."

"Have you?"

"Covertly. I'm good at that," she added. "The adoptive mother died when the child was eight, the same age Lisa was when her mother died. The father hasn't remarried, but he's been successful at what he does. They live in Miami, Florida, in a luxury condo."

Griffin held up the paper. "Does Heather have this?"

"No. There were times when I was tempted to share it, but I thought giving the child an identity might make it harder for her. For the most part, she doesn't think about the child. But on the anniversary of its birth, Heather gets melancholy. She never says why, but I can tell. That's the day when she seeks me out, even just for a cup of tea. She needs to be with family that day."

Poppy wanted to go to Florida. She knew it the minute Griffin told her about Heather's child. She didn't travel easily; she hadn't been on a plane since before the accident. But if Heather couldn't be there to talk with the child, she had to do it for her.

Cassie, whom they called at first light with the news, wasn't sure that a trip was necessary. She had a friend with a law firm in Miami who would gladly meet with the family and do the asking. After all, what did they need? A mouth swab? A strand of hair?

Griffin, on the other hand, would have flown to Miami himself had it not been for the ice storm. After protecting

Camille's identity by crediting Ralph with finding the child, he felt that he had a right to take the investigation to this next step. But there was work to be done in Lake Henry, and it wouldn't wait. Fallen limbs had to be cleared, and not only from the section of mainline Micah and he had focused on the night before. The entire sugar bush had to be scoured, downed wood removed, and damaged tubing repaired.

Griffin drove to the sugar bush early Monday morning. Poppy was behind him in the Blazer. This time they weren't the only ones coming down Micah's drive. Pete Duffy was already there, quickly joined by Charlie Owens and his two oldest boys; John Kipling; Rose's husband, Art Winslow; and nine other burly men from town. All had chain saws, crampons, and thermoses of coffee.

Griffin was as gratified that they'd come as he was by the humble look Micah wore each time another truck pulled up. None of the men said much. It was too early and their task too urgent. They broke into teams of four and set off up the hill.

Poppy watched from the back door. The last of the men and their white puffs of breath had disappeared when the women began to arrive, and none came empty-handed. The kitchen quickly filled with food and the kind of quiet talk that Poppy found to be as soothing as the lake on a warm summer night.

When the men returned for lunch, the kitchen table was piled with sandwiches and bowls of soup. On the positive side, the men had finished removing debris from the crucial portion of mainline that had split, and they could have the line repaired by the end of the day. On the negative side, there was enough other damage to warrant two more days of work in the woods.

• • •

Cassie spent part of Monday afternoon in her car, talking on her cell phone while the engine charged it up. She went back and forth between the assistant attorney general in Sacramento and her law school friend in Miami. In the end, she struck out with both.

That evening she explained the dilemma to those remaining at Micah's house. "The adoptive father, Norman Anderson, may be a problem," she said. "My law school friend says Norman is a decent man who has made a lot of money over the years as the president and chairman of the board of a group of banks in the southern U.S. He's a quiet, private person who values that privacy above everything else—except his daughter. He adores her. Apparently, they were always close but became even more so when his wife died. He absolutely will not want publicity from something like this."

"But if Anderson works with us," Griffin argued, "won't he be able to control the publicity? His daughter's confidentiality will be guaranteed, won't it?"

Cassie nodded. "That's what we'll argue. My friend has a meeting with him set up for tomorrow. She wants to tell him about Heather. She feels that if they lay things out for him, there's a chance he'll be sympathetic to our position."

"What kind of chance do we have?" Poppy asked Cassie.

"Fifty-fifty, maybe."

"What if you were there?" Poppy asked. "Would it help?"

"I offered. My friend felt too many lawyers would turn Anderson off."

"What about me, then?" Poppy asked. "I'm not a lawyer. I'm an ordinary person."

"Poppy, you don't travel that way," Maida said.

"But what if I did?" Poppy turned back to Cassie. "What

if I was there to give Heather a personal face? Would it help?"

Cassie smiled crookedly. "It wouldn't hurt. You're certainly not threatening."

"I evoke sympathy."

"I did not say that."

"Well, I *do*," Poppy insisted. "I've never used my disability before, but in this instance I don't care. If my traveling that distance in a wheelchair makes Norman Anderson think about Heather as a human being, I'll do it."

Griffin put a hand on her shoulder. "Wait a few days. Once the sugar bush is cleared, I'll go with you."

But Poppy shook her head. "This won't wait. I need to do this," she said with quiet confidence. Her eyes were on Maida.

Before the accident, Poppy had traveled at the drop of a hat. She hadn't had to worry about wheelchair travel or about finding herself in a strange place with no one to help. Now she thought about both of those things, and they frightened her. But just because she was frightened of something didn't mean she shouldn't try.

Griffin was silent. He understood. And Maida?

She studied her daughter for a long moment, then crossed the short distance, bent down, and gave Poppy a hug.

Griffin drove Poppy to Manchester early Tuesday morning for the six-forty-five flight to Miami. Once they got to the airport, he set her in her chair, put her carry-on over his shoulder, and wheeled her inside. When they reached the security point, he hunkered down with his hands framing her chair. "Do you have money?"

"Yes."

"Credit card? Change of underwear? Meds?"

"Yes, but only because you hounded me into it. I'm coming

back tonight. I land at eleven forty-two. The meeting at the law firm is set for one thirty. If I don't make the four-nineteen flight, there's another at six thirty. That gets me here at eleven fifty-four. Can't I just take a taxi back to Lake Henry?"

"No," he said in a way that brooked no argument. "Are you nervous about flying?"

"I'm nervous about the whole thing." When he leaned toward her, she hung a hand around his neck. "Why don't you leave now? I have to get in line, and you have to be at the sugar bush."

"I can wait with you."

"You can't. You don't have time. I'm okay, Griffin. I really am."

He rose, kissing her halfway up. "I know you are, dollface. That's the problem. I'm worried you'll find out just how okay you are and forget that I'm waiting for you here." Smiling, he straightened and put the carry-on in her lap. He backed off, turned and walked away, turned again and walked backward for a bit with his eyes on her, only her, and all the while she watched.

The flight was smoother than Poppy remembered flying to be. She had planned well—had limited her intake of fluid and used the airport bathroom prior to boarding so that she didn't have to use the lav on board. Once she was in her seat and strapped in, she felt like everyone else.

When the plane taxied up to the jetport in Miami, Cassie's friend Susan McDermott was waiting at the gate. She came forward with a smile as soon as Poppy wheeled into the terminal, and she led her out to a waiting car. They were quickly on their way into the city.

Poppy took it all in—warm air, palm trees, a skyline of buildings rather than hills—but what she felt most was the satisfaction of having gotten this far. She let that pleasure buoy her as she wheeled into the elevator in the law firm's building, but it dwindled as she followed Susan down to a mahogany-appointed conference room.

Norman Anderson was older than Poppy had pictured. He looked vulnerable, which would have surprised her if she hadn't been even more surprised by his companion. One look at her and Poppy lost her breath. She didn't need an introduction.

Althea Anderson didn't have her mother's silver eyes, certainly not that telltale scar, but the resemblance was everywhere else. Mother and daughter had the same long, thick hair, the same heart-shaped face, straight eyebrows, and slight build.

Poppy couldn't take her eyes off the child. Child? Thea was fourteen going on twenty-two. She was gently developed, sweetly curved, and dressed in a miniskirt and sweater that were surprisingly discreet. Her whole manner was refined.

Poppy nodded in acknowledgment as the introductions were made, but her eyes stayed on Thea. "I'm sorry," Poppy finally said to her, because she was feeling choked up. "You are just so much like your mother. You're very beautiful."

"Thank you," Thea whispered with a tentative smile.

Susan gave a description of the case Cassie was hoping to make on behalf of Heather. Then the lawyers went back and forth—about legalities, about confidentiality, about juvenile rights. Poppy listened, but her eyes kept returning to Thea. The girl didn't seem as interested in what the lawyers were saying as Poppy thought she would be. Then she realized that Thea had heard it all before. There was no surprise here. What there was, was curiosity. If Poppy were to guess, the girl wanted to know about Heather.

Her father was quiet, leaving it to his lawyer to counter

Susan's plea for immediate cooperation. The Andersons' lawyer argued against rushing when it came to involving a child like Thea.

Involving a child like Thea? Poppy couldn't let the statement go unchallenged. "I'm surprised she's here now. I would have thought you would want to shield her even from this."

Norman Anderson answered, "Thea has a mind of her own. She's been following this case in the news. She wanted to be here."

"Has she always known who her biological parents are?"

"She's always known she was adopted. I hadn't realized she knew the identity of her birth mother until a few days ago."

When Thea slid him a guilty look, Poppy decided against asking the details of that. "Heather has a mind of her own, too," Poppy told the girl. "She wouldn't tell any of us that she'd had a child, because she didn't want to involve you in this. We had to get your name from someone else, because she doesn't know it. She came to Lake Henry with nothing of her past except a letter from the law firm that handled the adoption—and this." She dug the tiny plastic ID bracelet from her bag and held it out over the table.

"I don't think that's appropriate," the Andersons' lawyer began. It became a moot point when Thea took the bracelet and studied it.

The lawyers continued to argue back and forth. When neither side would budge, Susan suggested they take a break.

Poppy wheeled herself down the hall to the ladies' room. She had just emerged from the largest stall and was approaching the sink when Thea slipped into the room and eased the door closed.

Her eyes were filled with curiosity. "Is she beautiful?" she asked.

Poppy nodded. "She is. Wait." She washed and dried her hands, then pulled pictures from her bag. Watching Thea's face as she turned from one to the next was a sight in itself.

"She's happy in these," the girl said.

"She has a happy life. She's a lovely person, Thea—beautiful inside and out—and she would do absolutely nothing to hurt you."

"You said she didn't know my name. Doesn't she want to?"

Poppy knew Heather well enough to answer. "She wants to, but she knows it's not smart. Letting you go was too painful. Knowing your name would make you real, and then she would want to know more. You have your own life. She won't intrude on that."

Sounding more her age, Thea said, "I snuck the adoption papers from Mom's drawer right after she died. I thought my dad would be upset, so I didn't say anything until this week, but I knew he was following the news, and I wanted him to know I was, too."

"He seems like a wonderful man."

"He is. He's so cool. Like letting me come here today. A lot of parents wouldn't do that. I watched all the stuff about your town."

"We're in the middle of a crisis right now. We had an ice storm that may ruin the maple sugar season."

Thea singled out a photo of Heather and Micah. "His business?"

"Hers, too. She's his muse."

Thea leaned against the sink. "Tell me about a day in Heather's life—like, what time she gets up, what she has for breakfast."

Susan opened the ladies' room door and murmured a discreet "There's a little concern out here."

Poppy could have gone on for a while. She felt the same rapport with Thea that she had always felt with Heather. But the girl was fourteen, and the current meeting was supposed to be protecting her from the past. Though Poppy didn't think she needed protecting, she didn't want to create tension between Thea and her father.

"Okay. I'd better start back," she said, and wheeled out.

Chapter Ten

While Susan called Cassie with the good news, Poppy left the firm with the Andersons.

"Would you like to see where I live?" Thea had asked at the end of the meeting, and Poppy couldn't have possibly said no. Thea hadn't asked out of politeness; there was genuine eagerness there. Poppy shared the eagerness. She wanted to see as much as she could so that she would have answers if Heather asked.

Norman Anderson had a uniformed driver who drove a town car. Poppy and Thea sat in back, with Poppy's chair and carry-on in the trunk. Poppy saw the house where Thea had spent her younger years, saw the park where Thea's mother had taken her to play, saw the stores where they had shopped. When the car turned in at the gates of the community where Thea and her father lived, Poppy had already given up on making the four-nineteen flight.

"I think I need to call my guy," Poppy said, and dug into her bag for the phone.

"What's his name?" Thea asked with enthusiasm.

"Griffin. Griffin Hughes. He actually lives in New Jersey, but he's been in Lake Henry helping Micah out with sugaring, what with Heather not there and all." She punched out the number.

"Hey," Griffin said.

Poppy grinned and lowered her voice for a little privacy. "Hey yourself. Did you hear?"

"Sure did. Congratulations, honey. You did good."

"It wasn't me," she said softly. "Is Micah pleased?"

"You bet. He's holding his breath that Cassie can make a deal. Meantime, Micah's making syrup again. The mainline's repaired and is carrying enough sap to boil, but because there's no electricity, Micah is doing the filtering by hand. Are you at the airport?"

Thea pointed as they pulled in at a low, sprawling house.

"No. I'll take the later plane. The Andersons are giving me the Cook's tour of their lives. We've just pulled up at their house. I have to run, Griffin. I'll call again on my way to the airport."

"Please. I love you," Griffin said.

She paused for a second. "Me, too." Before he could respond, she pushed the END button and dropped the phone into her bag.

Moments later, from her wheelchair, Poppy toured Thea's home. She saw the girl's bedroom, which was green, gold, and tasteful, and the kitchen, the living room, and the den. Thea introduced her to a maid and a cook along the way. When the tour was done, they went out to the patio and sat by the pool. Thea wanted to know anything and everything about Lake Henry, and Poppy wanted to know about Thea's favorite foods, favorite bands, favorite sports.

Soon it was time for Poppy to head for the airport, but

Thea wouldn't hear of it. "You can stay over, Poppy, can't you? We have a gorgeous guest room. Our travel agent can change your reservations. I have to be at school by eight, anyway. We can drop you at the airport, then go on to school."

"That'll mean a very early morning for you," Norman cautioned.

Thea shot him a look of dismay. "It's okay. I can't let Poppy go to the airport alone." She turned to Poppy. "Will you stay?"

Cassie called the attorney general of California. "There's been a new development on my end. I FedExed a package to you that contains letters of agreement and affidavits that lay out our case."

"Which is?" the man asked politely.

"We found the child," she said. "We have a signed agreement from her father allowing her to participate in DNA tests. Heather will submit to the tests also, so we'll be able to prove that she is the child's mother. We'll be petitioning to have tests done from blood on the clothing Rob DiCenza wore that night. If it turns out the child isn't Rob's, that's the end of it. If it turns out the other way, we have a whole other ball game."

There was a brief silence. Then he said quietly, "Go on."

"If the paternity issue falls into place, it gives credence to other arguments we've made that the DiCenzas have refuted. And then there's Aidan Greene. He was Rob's best friend. Since he never testified under oath, he can't be charged with perjury."

"He can be charged with giving misleading information in an investigation."

"He didn't. We have the transcripts to show it. Aidan answered every question that he was asked. If the investigators didn't ask the right ones, he can't be held liable for that."

"What's your argument? Spell it out, please. I don't have all day."

"We contend that Lisa Matlock was impregnated by Rob DiCenza. When she refused to get the abortion that he wanted, he threatened her life and that of the child at the fund-raiser that night. When she got into her car, her only thought was to get away from him. He came out of the dark and jumped in front of the car. She couldn't stop."

"She left the scene."

"She had no idea Rob was dead. She was terrified of him. The fact is, sir, we have a strong case, should this go to a jury. We have a dark night, lots of cars, and a drunk man running between them. We have a poor, powerless young woman taken advantage of by a privileged, politically powerful man. We have a relationship with physical abuse. If this case goes to trial, we'll put people on the stand testifying that Lisa wasn't the only woman Rob beat."

"Oh, for heaven's sake. What's the point? The boy is dead."

Cassie couldn't believe he'd said that. The remark was totally biased, totally unprofessional. "You're right. He's dead. This whole *case* should be dead, because Rob's death was nothing more than a tragic accident. That's what a jury will find, only to prove it, we'll have to bring up all the rest. Will the DiCenza family like that? I doubt it. But that's their problem. They certainly didn't have any trouble bad-mouthing Lisa Matlock—or now Heather Malone—in a very public way. They've looked for the limelight in this case, and that's where this new information will come out if we don't settle it within forty-eight hours. After that I'll have to go to the press."

"I can prevent that with a gag order."

Cassie refused to buckle. "Only one side of the story has come out. The other needs an airing. If it doesn't come out now, it'll come out in court before a jury. Ask if the DiCenzas want their son dragged through the mud. Ask if they want a financial claim made on them by a fourteen-year-old girl who may be their grandchild. If we don't get a deal by Thursday afternoon, that's what'll happen."

"What kind of deal do you want?" the attorney general asked.

Cassie had nothing to lose. "I want the case dropped."

"I can't do that. Not with a murder case."

"Of course you can. You can say that given the amount of time that's passed and the potential for fuzzy memories, there isn't enough evidence to convict. You can advise the family that it's in their best interest to let this case die. You save face by coming forward as the compassionate arbiter of the situation. The family saves face by saying that it is simply too painful for them to have to relive this tragedy. If you agree to drop the charges, my client will agree not to divulge anything related to Rob DiCenza or this case, but I want her released from prison as soon as we make our deal."

"I don't have the final say here," the man muttered.

Cassie understood that. "I know that you can be very persuasive when you want to. You can make the argument that a fourteen-year-old who has a loving adoptive family shouldn't have to relive the sins of her birth parents. I'll look forward to hearing from you."

Micah was sweating. He was so hot he thought he would die of it, as he poured off the last batch of syrup and carted the tank toward the filtering system he had rigged up. Granted, the heat in the sugarhouse was a good thing, what with the girls sleeping in a corner of the room. The house was cold, and now that everyone had gone home, there was no one to stoke the fire there. Missy and Star had their sleeping bags here and would stay as long as Micah did.

"How's this depth?" Griffin asked. He was standing over the finish pan, which was newly replenished with sap that was nearing the syrup stage. He was at the ready should anything start to foam.

Micah glanced over and nodded that it was fine, but quickly returned to the task at hand. He was behind in the process. Having to filter everything by hand was slowing up the works. Even with Griffin helping, he would be working past midnight. He needed the electricity back on for the filter press, but the power company wasn't promising help for another two or three days.

It took two hours before the day's sap had been boiled into syrup, filtered, poured into tins, and sealed. Micah sent Griffin home, then gently shook the girls awake. Star put her arms up. He set her on his hip. "Get the lantern, Missy, and stay close."

He guided Missy along the dark path. Once inside the house, she went right to bed and was asleep in minutes. Star left an arm around Micah's neck when he would have tucked her into bed.

"Daddy?" she whispered. "Does Momma have a baby?"

"She did once," he told her.

"What happened to it?"

"She couldn't take care of it, so she gave it to people who could."

"Did the baby cry when she gave it away?"

"I think the baby was too little to know."

"I'd cry if you gave me away."

He tightened his hold of her. "Well, I would never do that."

"Does Heather's baby miss her now?"

Micah didn't know. Nor did he know what Heather felt about it all. "The baby's almost grown up now, and she has her own daddy."

"Me, too, but I miss Momma. If she had to choose, would she choose that baby instead of us?"

"She'd choose us," Micah said. But he wasn't sure. Heather had a past now. Regardless of the outcome of Cassie's dealings, she was free to be Lisa again. He couldn't imagine her choosing to return to California. But how could he know for sure?

Wednesday morning, instead of going to Micah's, Griffin went to the marina, switched the truck for his Porsche, and headed for Manchester. He was there earlier than he needed to be.

Poppy's plane was late. Griffin's eyes were on the arrival board when E.T.A. changed to IN. Eyes on the jetway, he waited for Poppy to come out. She was the last one to emerge, but the wait was worth it. The sight of her made his heart swell.

He started forward and bent over to hug her. When her arms went tight around his neck, he scooped her up and whirled her around. She was laughing by the time he set her back in her seat.

"Did you mean it?" He was talking about the words, of course.

She nodded. "Don't know what I'm going to do with it yet."

"We'll figure that out," he said, feeling giddy. "Come on. I want to introduce you to someone."

He pushed her chair through the terminal and into the parking lot. She spotted the Porsche before they reached it. "Someone?"

"She's inside."

He steadied her wheels while she shifted into the passenger seat of the Porsche; then he put her chair and carry-on in the trunk.

After Griffin slid behind the wheel, Poppy pointed to the GPS monitor. "Is this her?"

There went his surprise. "How did *you* know?"

She grinned. "We use these things on the lake. It helps finding our way through the islands at night. Charlie calls his Amelia."

Griffin sighed. "Mine's Sage. You just know too much, Poppy Blake. I can't surprise you with anything." As he turned the key in the ignition, Poppy closed a hand on his arm.

"You surprise me," she said, very serious now. "You're here."

Heart clenching, he nearly went for his pocket. He had something there, and it wasn't a kiss. But the timing wasn't right yet.

As Wednesday afternoon settled into Wednesday evening and no call came from California, Griffin began to think about how people in town would deal with a less than satisfactory outcome in Heather's case. Although he had done the best he could in helping to put together her case, if the California authorities rejected a deal and Heather had to face a nightmare of a trial, the goodwill he had established in Lake Henry could be reversed.

But he liked it here. He felt safe here. Lake Henry was the first place where the thought of raising children appealed to him. It was the first place he'd been in love—with a woman, a way of life. He could freelance from here, could work out of Poppy's house or rent space at the *Lake News* office. He didn't lack intellectual stimulation. People like Cassie, John, and Lily—they were as sophisticated as people anywhere. And Poppy? She was everything he wanted.

He didn't want to think that her love was contingent on the outcome of Heather's case, but he was a realist. If Heather's case went on and on and ended in a less than satisfactory way, Poppy might always remember that he had been the one responsible.

It was rather like her accident. Shift a few inches to the right or the left, and things might never be the same.

Thursday morning the lights went back on. By midday the phones were also back. At her office, Cassie kept an eye on the clock. She had given the attorney general of California forty-eight hours. As that time approached without a call, she felt a sinking in her stomach. Griffin arrived just as the phone rang.

"I'm making progress," the attorney general said, "but I need more time. The DiCenzas are having trouble with the idea that the woman who ran down their son will walk away free."

"How much more time did you have in mind?" Cassie asked.

"Another forty-eight hours."

"If that was their suggestion," Cassie remarked, "I'd say what they're doing is trying to push this off so that nothing will hit the papers over the weekend, when more people are at home and reading all the fine print. I'm sorry. I can't do forty-eight hours. I can do twenty-four. I'll give you until Friday at five, your time. If they haven't agreed by then, I'll have to hold a news conference. There will be plenty of time for coverage in Sunday's paper."

"You're tough."

"With due respect, sir, I'm only doing what you would do if you were representing a client who has already been punished ten times over for what was truly a tragic accident."

Griffin had barely set off from Cassie's office in the truck when his cell phone rang. Thinking it would be Poppy, he said, "Hey."

"What's going on there?" Prentiss Hayden asked. "I'm getting phone calls from mutual DiCenza friends. What's brewing?"

"The DiCenzas' past is coming back to haunt them."

"Rob was a good boy, and he's dead. Why go after a dead boy?"

"I won't comment on that," Griffin said. "But it's what I've been telling you for weeks. If you hide things, they'll come out sooner or later. On the other hand, if you come clean in your bio, no one has anything on you. You've picked the time, the place, the method. You've taken control rather than letting someone else do it."

"The existence of my son is between him and me."

"Normally, that'd be true. But you're a public figure. If you don't mention your son in this book, someone else will."

"Yes. It's just that I . . . Well, how would *you* feel if you'd led a successful and productive life and then someone wants to focus on a foolish little thing you did in your youth?"

"I don't think your son is foolish. He's a husband and a father. He's a pediatrician. I'd think you would be proud of that."

"I am. But it's such an intimate thing."

Griffin sighed. "Let's be honest here. Most people know he exists. His mother's dead, so she wouldn't be hurt, and your wife knows about him. He wasn't planned, but you handled it well. You made the most of it. That would be inspiring for people."

There was a grumbled "Do you think?"

"Definitely. People look up to you. This will only add to that."

There was a silence on the other end, then a sigh. After what seemed an eternity, Prentiss Hayden muttered a begrudging "Oh, do it," and hung up the phone.

• • •

Griffin cooked dinner for Poppy, then rebuilt the fire and settled her on the sofa in his arms. He told her about Prentiss. Then he said, "You're one of the lucky ones. The past is out there on the table now. The people who would judge you know the truth, and they still love you, so what do you say? Marry me, Poppy."

Poppy put her fingers over his mouth. "Don't ask that. Not yet."

"I love you."

"Now. But what about next week? Or next month?"

"What about next year? Or five years from now? Poppy, that's not the way it works. If people put their lives on hold while they waited to see if love lasted, they'd miss out on it completely."

"This has just happened so fast."

"Good things do. So why wait?"

"I don't know. There's still something . . ."

"Forgiving yourself? Why can't we be married while you work on it? What better person to help than your husband?"

"My husband? That is just such a dream."

"Make it come true."

She laced her fingers through his, studied all ten for a minute, then looked up. "Give me a little more time. Just a little more time. There's still something . . . I need to do."

On Friday, Cassie's phone rang at eight on the nose—five o'clock in California. It was her office line, which Poppy had rerouted to the house. Heart racing, she picked it up. "Yes?"

"They've agreed," said the attorney general, sounding tired.

Cassie smiled, closed her eyes, and let out a breath.

"They've agreed to dropping the charges," the attorney general went on, "but they want a nondisclosure agreement, and they want her back here in front of the judge for the dismissal."

"Why back there?" Cassie asked.

"They need closure," he said. "They feel that if the case disappears from the radar screen without any public explanation, it will raise questions. If there's a hearing at which we explain that we do not have the evidence to convict, the family can follow it up with a press conference honoring the memory of their son, explaining that vengeance won't bring him back and that it's time to put the case to rest. It's a face-saving thing, Ms. Byrnes. Give them this."

"If you're asking us to sign a nondisclosure agreement," she said, "I'm afraid we'll need the same. I won't have my client returning to a hostile place where she'll be talked about as a killer who beat the system. I'd rather go to trial and have the whole story come out."

From the other end of the line came an exasperated "I can't control what the press does. I can't do anything about public opinion."

"Yes, you can. You can settle this quietly. Heather can appear before a magistrate in New Hampshire. The charges can be dropped. She'll sign away the right to talk about Rob if the DiCenzas sign away the right to talk about her. That's a fair deal."

There was a pause, then an almost admiring "You are tough."

"Yup," Cassie said with a grin.

Ten minutes later she got the call she wanted. She promptly called Micah, then Poppy and Griffin. And Camille, because she knew that something was special there. She didn't want to know what it was. It was enough that this was one more person who cared about Heather.

Chapter Eleven

Saturday dawned glorious. The sun rose a pale yellow and grew bolder as it climbed.

Micah had gone to the impromptu party at Charlie's Café the night before, but only because Camille came to sit with the girls and practically kicked him out. He stayed only long enough to thank the people who had done so much for him, though, before heading home. He spent most of the night lying in bed awake, feeling Heather beside him.

He hadn't told the girls about Cassie's deal. He hadn't wanted to contend with the questions about when she would be home. He didn't know when, because Cassie didn't know when. She had mentioned magistrates, paperwork, and hearings. Besides, Heather coming home was one thing. Her staying there was another. Micah wouldn't know which she would choose until the moment arrived.

When morning came, Micah gave the girls breakfast, dressed them warmly, loaded them in the tractor, and took them into the sugar bush. Stopping the tractor, he lifted them down and led them through the snow to a boulder. It was one he had gone to as a child when he wanted to be alone. It was quiet, untouched, peaceful land.

He lifted the girls onto the boulder one at a time. Then he climbed up between them. He didn't say anything. The trees were tall here—mossy pines, deep green hemlocks, and blue firs. A startling number of limbs lay fallen under the weight of ice.

"God's pruning?" Missy asked, and he nodded.

Star whispered, "Shh. Listen." The woods were alive with snow-melt, a gentle dripping that came from different sections of nature's orchestra, each with its own tempo and tone, all harmonizing. Her eyes held the light of excitement. "Snow songs."

God's pruning. Nature's orchestra. Snow songs. They were all Heather's expressions. She put into words what Micah felt but couldn't say. Her words would live on in all of them, regardless of what she did herself.

They sat that way for a long time, the girls seemingly as content as he was. Eventually he herded them back to the tractor and drove them down the hill. By the time they reached the sugarhouse, the driveway was lined with trucks.

Lake Henry had come to make sugar.

Poppy arrived at Micah's well after the first of the other trucks had pulled in. Once she had parked, she and Griffin unloaded the huge pot of chili that they'd picked up at Charlie's. The problem was finding room in the kitchen, which was even more packed with food and people than it had been after the ice storm.

She felt an intense pride. This was her town; these were her people. They did this each year to celebrate the sap harvest—picked a day when the sun was out, the air was clear, and the children had no school, because, like Christmas, sugar-on-snow was best with kids.

Micah smiled more in the ten minutes he had spared for lunch than he had in the last twenty-four days. Then he headed for the sugarhouse with dozens of people in tow. Griffin was already there, bringing wood in. Poppy whipped out the front door and down the ramp. She pushed her wheels through the last of the ice that was melting on the drive and joined the back of the procession.

Far ahead of her, at the foot of the hill, Micah opened the sugarhouse door and turned to hold it for those behind him. In the process he glanced toward the road. His body went still. Only his eyes moved, following something down the drive.

Heart pounding, Poppy looked that way. It was a dark red car, late model, not from Lake Henry. The car moved slowly, then pulled up just shy of the house. Even before the driver opened his door, the pounding of Poppy's heart increased.

She pushed herself forward, separating from the others just as Norman Anderson straightened. He caught her eye right away. The look said that he wouldn't have shown up here unannounced if his headstrong fourteen-year-old daughter hadn't forced the issue.

Sure enough, Thea had left the passenger's seat and was rounding the front of the car. Her face spoke of both excitement and terror. When she caught sight of Poppy, she seemed relieved.

Not so Poppy. She had been proud of herself to have instantly connected with Heather's daughter. It struck her now, though, that the connection might well have been responsible for bringing Thea here at such a bad time. She couldn't begin to think of what would happen if Heather arrived just then.

Poppy wheeled quickly forward, and Norman met her

halfway. "I'm sorry," he said in a low voice. "If I'd said no, Thea would have come here on her own. She wanted to meet Micah. She wanted to take a look at the town. I thought we could do it without anyone knowing who we are." He shot a look at the crowd. "I guess not."

Thea put an arm around Poppy's shoulder and kissed her cheek. While she was there, she murmured, "Did I do an awful thing?"

They didn't know about the plea agreement, Poppy realized with a start. She was thinking that it was going to be the three of them—Norman, Thea, and her—against Lake Henry, when Griffin materialized beside her and offered a hand.

"Mr. Anderson, I'm Griffin Hughes. Welcome."

"Thank you," Norman said.

Poppy imagined that he was as relieved to see Griffin as she was.

"Relieved" wasn't a word Micah would have used. He felt just the opposite. He wanted Heather back there, choosing this life before any child of hers appeared, but he could tell it was too late for that. He didn't need an introduction to know that the young woman with Poppy was Heather's daughter. She was a young, elegant version of Heather.

Needing to hold what was his, he looked around for Missy and Star. He saw Missy first as she headed for the house. When Maida went after her, he looked for Star. It was a frightened minute before he saw her emerge from the crowd and walk toward Poppy.

Unable to think of anything but that he was losing everything that mattered to him, he followed and was beside them in a few long strides. He stopped behind Star, with challenging eyes on Norman, and Poppy had a sudden fear that he would lash out.

Poppy gave his arm a squeeze through his flannel sleeve and turned to Thea. "This is Micah. It's an emotional day for him because we don't know when Heather will be getting back. So we're keeping ourselves busy by celebrating the sugar season. Micah has sap to boil. Maybe you'd like to watch."

Thea smiled at Micah and said softly, "I would really like that."

Poppy looked up at Micah. This was his house, his land, his sap. Heather might be the one to decide whether she wanted an ongoing relationship with Thea, but he was the one to decide, here and now, whether the girl and her father stayed.

Before he could say anything, Star looked up at Thea and slowly, carefully, put a hand in hers. Seeming utterly sure of what she was doing, she raised her eyes to Micah.

After that, of course, Micah had no more say in the matter than Norman had when Thea had threatened to fly to Lake Henry by herself. Micah did not want Thea to exist. But she did. She was part of Heather, whom he loved. Even if Star hadn't led the way, he doubted he would have been able to ask her to leave.

He also loved Missy, and Missy was upset. Needing to see her, he motioned the others on to the sugarhouse while he went back into the house. He found Missy in her bedroom with Maida.

"We were just talking about things," Maida said with a little smile. "Missy needs to vent."

"She kept secrets," Missy charged, scowling.

Micah didn't know what to say. Missy had a point. But the fact was, he hadn't asked about the things Heather had kept to herself. He had built a life with Heather and had gone right along with the idea that the past didn't matter. So maybe he was at fault, too.

He said, "We'll talk about it once she's back."

"I don't want her back."

"I do. I love her. We all make mistakes. We have to forgive her."

Missy's chin trembled. "I don't."

"Then you lose her. Is that what you want?"

Missy didn't answer.

"We're doing sugar-on-snow. Don't you want some?"

That eased her pout a bit. "I don't know. Maybe."

"I'm going to go make it." He held out a hand. When she simply stared at him, he dropped it. "Come over when you're ready."

Micah began boiling the sap that had just run, and it took concentration. He didn't think about Heather. He didn't think about Thea. He knew that the sugarhouse was packed with people and that others were outside packing snow in plastic soup bowls, pie plates, and foil pans. The first batch of sap quickly became syrup. He let it boil, constantly stirring. Shortly before it reached the point where it would be high and dry enough to beat into granular sugar, he poured it off into buckets—two for him, two for Griffin. Leaving Billy at the evaporator, they went outside.

How not to feel good, then? He had barely set down his buckets when he was surrounded by children, each holding a container of snow. One at a time he ladled hot syrup on the snow in a swirling design, handed the container back, and went on to the next. When the syrup hit the snow, it cooled instantly and became chewy enough to be picked up with fingers. Eaten alone, it was delicious. Eaten between bites of doughnut and pickle, containers of which were waiting on a long table nearby, it was the best.

When Star came up with her plate of snow, Micah asked, "Where's your sister?"

She pointed. Missy was sitting with Rose's daughters, Emma and Ruth, and she seemed happy enough.

Relieved by that, he went back to work. Once the children had their fill, the adults came by, and then there were seconds until his buckets ran dry. He was thinking that he ought to go back inside, when far down the drive the Lake Henry police cruiser appeared.

As he set the buckets down, he felt a chill on the back of his neck—a premonition—much as he had that morning more than three weeks before. He figured it wasn't just him, because around him the laughter seemed to fade and the crowd quieted.

He started forward. The cruiser slowed and had barely come to a halt when the passenger door opened.

Micah did stop then, but only until he saw Heather round the front of the car, pause for a single instant, then break into a run. Her coat flapped open; her hair flew to both sides. Even from the distance he could see that she was crying, but her eyes were a sparkling silver, her face alive with happiness—and she was coming to him, *running* to him. Suddenly he had no doubts. He didn't know why he ever had. What they shared didn't just go away.

He started to run, and then she was in his arms, sobbing his name. "I love you," she whispered. She drew back, hesitant at the last moment. "Can I come back? I want to come back."

He wiped the tears from her cheeks with his thumbs and kissed her with all his strength, all his passion. Then he crushed her to him, closed his eyes, and lifted her right off the ground and around.

When he set her down, she touched his cheek in that gentle way that she had. Then she whispered, "I need to see my girls."

Incredibly, her eyes held his, asking permission.

He glanced back at the crowd to see Star slipping through legs. She ran to Heather, who caught her up off the ground and hugged her nearly as hard as she had hugged Micah.

"Where's Missy?" Heather asked Star, who looked back toward the crowd. Missy was there on its edge, looking as though she could as easily run, stay, or cry.

Passing Star to Micah's arms, Heather crossed to where Missy stood. Micah didn't know if she spoke, he was too far away to hear, but he saw her tip her head and stroke Missy's hair.

Missy's chin trembled, and her eyes filled with tears. In a matter of seconds her face crumbled and she went forward, slipping her arms around Heather's waist, locking her hands behind.

Others closed in then, hugging Heather in turns, though Heather kept Missy pressed close through it all.

Pete Duffy came forward. "We pulled strings to get her today. It was the least we could do. You two need to be together."

Micah shook his hand. Still holding Star but needing to be near Heather, he joined the crowd. As soon as he was close enough, Heather slid an arm around him. It was the four of them then, standing on the land they owned, surrounded by people they loved. Right then, if Micah had been offered a million dollars for the land and five million for the business, he would have refused it. He had the richest life any man could want.

Taking a long, deep, easy breath, he looked up. There, standing distant and apart, respectful of Heather and Micah and the life they had, were the Andersons.

Feeling confident now, Micah took Heather's hand. "There's someone I want you to meet." While he held Star and Heather held Missy, he led her through the crowd. When they emerged on the sugarhouse side, Heather took in a sharp breath and stopped.

Thea didn't move. She looked terrified. It occurred to Micah that while he was frightened of losing Heather to this child, Thea was frightened that her birth mother wouldn't even want to *see* her.

He said quietly to Heather, "That's her dad with her. They adore each other, and they have a good life. But she wants to meet you."

Heather looked up at Micah. Her silver eyes were shimmering with tears. Again—incredibly—she was asking permission.

She could have asked for anything just then, and he'd have given it, he was that in love with her.

She must have seen it in his eyes because she seemed to calm some. Then, taking Missy along with her, she approached Thea.

After a long, full, emotional day, Poppy knew what she needed to do. While Griffin built a fire and manned the phones, she changed and went into the exercise room. It was time.

She did an upper-body workout, then used the recumbent bike. When she felt warmed up, she went to the wall where the leg braces hung. She hated everything about them, but they were the means to an end, and that end was the means to a beginning.

With the braces on her lap she wheeled back to the parallel bars, took a breath, and called out for Griffin.

He came to the door smiling. When he saw what she held,

his smile faded. His eyes found hers. She saw a question there. She imagined that she also saw hope. Buoyed by that, she held out the braces. "Strapping them on takes a little effort. Will you help?"

Four weeks later she set off on her own. She didn't say where she was going. She left Griffin writing the final pages of the Hayden biography, preoccupied enough to assume she was just running into town. As she drove away in the Blazer, she rolled down her window. April had come, bringing warm rains that turned every unpaved road to mud. Buds were starting to pop on the trees. Despite the mess underfoot, the air was earthy and full of promise.

Ice-out had occurred at two o'clock the afternoon before. Poppy had watched it from her deck, calling Griffin at the last minute when the ice just seemed to dissolve. By dusk Poppy had calls of two separate loon sightings. She had listened from her deck after that but hadn't heard a thing.

Her palms were clammy on the steering wheel. As nervous as she was, she refused to go back. Turning into the parking lot at the very center of town, Poppy went to the right of the church and started up the narrow cemetery road. It was paved, although only barely, and heavily puddled. She crested the small rise that led to Perry's grave, drove to a spot directly opposite, and parked.

She took the lift to the ground and reached back into the Blazer for her things. The left brace went on, then the right one. She was adept at it now, slowed only by nervous fingers.

Quickly, lest she lose her nerve, she pulled her crutches from the Blazer and slid her forearms into place, pulled herself forward in the wheelchair, and levered herself up. She shifted her weight onto her left leg, used her right hip to throw the right leg forward, shifted her weight onto that leg, drew the back leg forward, and let both share the weight. Taking a breath, she repeated the motion.

She did it again. And again. And again. She refused to look back, to think of the distance she was from her wheelchair. One step at a time—one clichéd step at a time—she crossed the graveyard.

What had been a raised slab of snow in February was now a stone bench. That was her goal. When she felt herself tiring—shoulders trembling, arms aching, hips threatening to spasm—she looked at the bench. The farther she went, the harder she breathed. But the closer she got, the more determined she grew.

The last few steps were the hardest. Carefully, using her crutches for leverage, she lowered herself to the bench and set them down. It was a minute before she caught her breath.

Then, with a breath that shuddered for a whole other reason, she looked at the headstone. PERRY WALKER, it read. BELOVED SON AND FRIEND, HERE TOO SHORT A TIME.

As she stared at the inscription—read and reread it—her throat grew tight. When her eyes filled with tears that blurred the words, she imagined she saw Perry's face in the granite.

"I'm sorry," she whispered brokenly. "I am so very sorry." Tears came then, and she didn't fight them. Grasping the edge of the bench, she cried for Perry and his family and all they had lost. She cried for her own family and all she had put them through. And she cried for herself—for the loss of her childhood and her athleticism, for the loss of a certain innocence and daring after that night twelve years before. She cried until she ran out of tears. Then, without speaking aloud, she told Perry where she'd been and what she'd done since she'd seen him last, knowing he would hear somehow.

Finally she closed her eyes, bowed her head, and recalled a prayer. It had to do with forgiveness.

A sound came. Eyes opening, she raised her head and listened. It was another minute before it came again, but the wait was worth it. She felt cleansed. Along with that feeling came a certain calm.

With a last look at Perry's grave, she picked up the crutches and slid her forearms in. Turning on the bench to gauge the return walk, she glanced back at the Blazer. Griffin stood beside it.

She should have been surprised, but she wasn't. He was attuned to her needs. He must have known why she had wanted to walk and where she was headed today. Seeing him there, she was nearly as overcome with emotion as she had been facing Perry. For Perry it had been sorrow she felt. For Griffin it was love. Seeing him there, she was so full of joy that she thought her heart might burst.

He didn't move. He didn't rush forward to take her arm or pick her up or express concern, though she did see concern on his face. But he was telling her that he had faith in her. He knew she could do this. He knew she could do most anything she set her mind to. And in that instant she thought he might be right.

She began to walk. Her gait was as faltering as it had been on the way out, but the awkwardness was irrelevant now, because she wasn't looking at a gravestone. She wasn't looking at the past. She was looking at the present and the future, and that was Griffin.

Only when she was under way did he begin to walk toward her, and then he did it slowly, matching his relaxed pace to hers. She loved him more with every single uneven step she took.

He met her halfway. Then he stood there, not touching her. "I am so in love with you I can't stand it," he said.

She started to laugh. He couldn't have said anything better.

He grinned, but the concern lingered in his eyes. It struck her then that the concern didn't have to do with whether she could walk through the mud on her own.

"I have something in my pocket," he said, and she knew he wasn't talking about a kiss.

"Can I see?" she asked, suddenly *dying* to see.

He stepped closer. "Reach in."

Adjusting her crutches, she put a hand in his pocket. There was only one thing there. She caught her breath.

"Take it out," he whispered.

Her hand emerged with the ring on the tip of her finger. He slid it on the rest of the way, then let her look, and she gasped. The diamond was emerald cut and exquisite, flanked by single baguettes.

Poppy could barely breathe. "It's *gorgeous*," she whispered, and suddenly she was tired of standing. She threw her arms around Griffin's neck as the crutches fell to the ground. He picked her up.

"Gorgeous isn't yes or no," he said against her hair.

"Yes. Yes!" she cried, but another cry echoed it. It was one she had heard a short time before, risen from the lake to mark a rebirth.

The loons had returned to Lake Henry.

About the Author

She loves lobster and strawberry shortcake. She is passionately in love with her husband, to whom she has been married for nearly thirty-five years. She does her best creative thinking in the car. Is it any wonder that Barbara Delinsky's millions of fans see her as a strong, likable, down-to-earth woman—just like the heroines in her books?

Describing herself as "an everyday woman who writes about everyday people facing not-so-everyday challenges," Delinsky started writing fiction as a stay-at-home mother raising three young sons. "It was a wonderful way to pass the hours," she says. "I could supervise them while I kept a pad of paper on my lap and wrote." Now, more than twenty years later, she is a publishing phenomenon. She attributes her success to the close relationship she has forged with her audience. In fact, *An Accidental Woman* was partly inspired by readers who wanted to know more about Poppy and Griffin, two characters introduced in Delinsky's 1999 novel, *Lake News*.

Delinsky and her husband divide their time between homes in suburban Boston and rural New Hampshire.

IF YOU LIKED THIS BOOK, YOU'LL ENJOY THESE:

Lake News by Barbara Delinsky

Distant Shores by Kristin Hannah

Envy by Sandra Brown

Handyman by Linda Nichols

Breathing Room by Susan Elizabeth Phillips

My Mother's Daughter by Judith Henry Wall

DID YOU KNOW...

- Barbara Delinsky has written seventy books, and more than twenty million copies of her books are now in print worldwide.
- When Barbara Delinsky began her writing career, she wrote under the pseudonyms Bonnie Drake and Billie Douglass.
- Barbara Delinsky and her husband share their home with a beloved tortoiseshell cat named Chelsea, who can often be found in the sunny office where Delinsky pens her best-selling books.